"In a journey that spans time and memory, focuses pain to a point of light in the brokenness of the world, and resolves toward grace, Terry Trueman has delivered a novel of uncommon perspective. Encapsulated in the wreckage of modern life, a subtle friendship is formed that transcends generational trauma, releases a heart's-cry elegy to Bukowski and Whitman, and symbolizes the poem that resides in the heart of everyman."
—Shann Ray, American Book Award winning author of *Balefire*, *American Masculine*, and the poetry chapbook *Atomic Theory 432*

"Every aspiring young author will benefit from this book. Packed with wit and wisdom, *The Kid Who Killed Cole Hardt* entertains, illuminates and inspires."
—Michael Gurian, *New York Times* bestselling author of *The Wonder of Boys*

"I love this kind of novel – fast-moving, unabashedly intelligent, darkly funny. Classic Terry Trueman, in other words. Coming-of-age sometimes takes a knock upside the head, and by the end, Trueman's "kid" is anything but a kid. This book is perfect for that bright, next generation of readers and leaders looking to take the wheel. Literally and metaphorically, Trueman hands over the keys."
—Will Weaver, award-winning author of *Memory Boy*

"Another great story by Terry Trueman, whose books always hit squarely on issues of coming of age and learning important life lesson
—Edward Ave

D1311026

THE KID WHO KILLED COLE HARDT

Also by Terry Trueman

Fiction
Stuck in Neutral
Inside Out
Cruise Control
No Right Turn
7 Days at the Hot Corner
Hurricane
Life Happens Next
Gettin' Weird
M.C. Idol: The Funniest Kid in the World

Non-Fiction
What Stories Does My Son Need?
Boys and Girls Learn Differently! (Co-authored
with Michael Gurian)

Poetry
Sheehan: Heartbreak and Redemption
Huge House
Where's the Fire?
Where We Going with This?
Clawing at the Door, Scratching at the Window

The Kid Who Killed Cole Hardt

Terry Trueman

Latah Books
Spokane, Washington

The Kid Who Killed Cole Hardt
Copyright © 2018 Terry Trueman

Cover design by Marina Gulova

ISBN: 978-0-9997075-4-8
Cataloging-in-Publication Data is available upon request

Manufactured in the United States of America

Book design and production by Gray Dog Press
4|19c   www.graydogpress.com

Published by
Latah Books, Spokane, Washington
www.latahbooks.com

The author may be contacted at:
ttrueman1215@msn.com

Dedicated to the memory of Charles Bukowski.
"What matters most is how well you walk
through the fire."

And for Stephanie Squicciarini,
a great friend much beloved.

I always wanted to be rich and famous, but now nothing matters to me. Nothing will ever matter to me again—not that I probably have all that much time left anyway. My life is over. Kaput. Finito. Done. Period. Exclamation point.

I'm screwed.

Coleman 'Cole' Hardt, the world-famous celebrity and the man many people, myself included, consider the greatest American writer of this century, looks over at me and smiles.

"Look at it this way, Ryan," he says. "Even if you never do anything else for the rest of your life, you'll be remembered as the kid who killed Cole Hardt."

He starts to laugh but stops, grimacing in pain and grabbing his left leg.

Then he passes out.

2

Cole and I are upside down in my dad's 2003 Corvette.
We're at the bottom of a steep drop, maybe ten or twelve
feet below the side of the road. We *were* on State Highway
54 that runs between Eastern Washington and North
Idaho (AKA the ultimate Nowhereville, USA). It's a road
that hardly anyone ever uses. We're a good thirty, maybe
even forty, feet back towards the woods. With the car
being upside down, the black undercarriage and the black
tires of the Corvette are facing upwards towards the sky,
which must make us look like we're part of the dark forest
floor.

This car, my dad's most prized possession, is *Le Mans
Blue*, a dark color that looks black at night. The dark blue
fiberglass body—what's left of it anyways—is buried in the
tall bushes and wild shrubs where we landed a few moments
ago. Even in the daylight, it's unlikely that someone driving
by on the road above would see us. And they definitely

won't see us at night, which is fast approaching. We might as well be invisible.

Over these last few minutes, I've checked the door handles and glanced at the car's windows and the front and back glass. I've been trying to find some way out of here, but the doors are mashed tight against the frame and the ground. And although the glass is broken out, the top of the Corvette—which is underneath us now—is smashed down so low that I can't possibly squeeze through and go for help. We're stuck, trapped.

Did I mention that I'm totally screwed?

When we crashed, Cole got tossed out of his seat and is now stuck sitting on what used to be the top of the car. He is bent over in an uncomfortable position. But at least he's sitting upright. I'm still belted into my seat upside down.

Also, we're both hurt.

Hardt has a cut on his forehead. It's not too deep or too bloody, but even in the dimming light I can see it.

He wakes up again and looks at me, forcing a smile. "How you doing?"

I take a breath and say, "Not too bad." Even before I finish my sentence, I let out a short cry as I try to move. It feels like somebody just stabbed me in my back, an intense pain a few inches to the left of my spine and halfway between the top of my ass and my shoulder. Thinking about my shoulder, I realize that it hurts like hell too.

"Where's the pain?" Hardt asks.

"I'm okay," I answer, groaning again.

"Bullshit! I'm the tough guy here. Where are you hurt?"

I tell him about my back and shoulder.

He nods. "Probably your ribs and collarbone."

"Are you okay?" I ask.

He smiles. "Nope."

"Sorry, stupid question," I say. "I can see that cut on your forehead."

"That's nothing," he says. "I've also got a shard of bone sticking up through my pant leg . . . I don't think that's a real good sign."

He laughs and grimaces and passes out again.

3

This situation is *bad*.

Okay, in spite of my injuries, at least I can think and I'm awake. I wiggle my toes, bend my arms, and squeeze my hands into fists. I seem to be mostly all right, not paralyzed or anything. My heart is pounding so hard in my chest that it feels like it might explode. I have to calm down, take a deep breath . . .

Ohhhh!

So much for deep breaths. That hurt like hell!

Okay, calm down. Think.

With Cole unconscious, it is eerily silent. Usually in the woods, especially at night, there're lots of sounds—animals and insects scurrying around, the wind moving through the trees and sounding a bit like a whispering voice. I can't hear any of those sounds right now. It's as if the forest knows that we don't belong here, like we're eavesdroppers trying to capture its secrets. The quiet is creepy. I wish Cole would wake up.

How did I get myself, get *us,* into this fix? What kind of a four-star, mini-brained-moron of sub-vertebrate must I be to have landed us in this predicament? How did it happen? Man, I don't know. Where do I even start?

I guess it all began with me deciding that I wanted to be famous someday. Yeah, I can totally admit this. The problem is that I can't draw, paint, cook, carve, dance, sculpt, sing, act, juggle, tightrope walk, bullfight, and obviously NASCAR or any activity requiring *driving skills* is out of the question. My only talent is making up stories, so that narrowed my options for fame and fortune down to the dream of becoming a wildly successful author.

Writing isn't easy for me, but it's the only thing I can do decently at all. I'm on Twitter and YouTube and Facebook. But to be honest, in a country of three hundred million people like the United States, having 26 people visit my YouTube poetry reading, getting 19 hits on my internet 'published' short stories page, and being 'followed' by 112 people I've never met face to face on Twitter, just isn't gonna cut it for me. When I talk about fame and fortune, what I'm saying is that I'd like everybody to know my name. Well, maybe not everybody, but a heck of a lot more than know it right now.

A lot of kids want to be famous because people who

aren't don't seem as important somehow. I know you're not supposed to say that—about normal people not mattering as much as famous ones—but I think most kids my age, if they were being honest, would agree. We like the idea of being important, of making our mark on the world.

Lots of kids these days want to reach fame by music. Rap is pretty cool, and I guess country music is okay too if you drive a pick-up truck and wear a cowboy hat. For the most part, the geezers still control rock and roll. Getting famous by being an actor on TV or in the movies seems cool too. Just think about it—if everybody recognizes your face, you'll get a lot more requests for autographs.

These are the paths most kids imagine taking to fame and celebrity, but I figure I'll get there by being a writer. How does that work? Just think about it. Writers create the scripts for movies and TV shows, write novels and articles, and get to be interviewed on cable channels and for major magazine stories about their fabulous lives. Writers get to win Pulitzer and Nobel Prizes and become rich and famous.

Not that many kids my age think of themselves as writers, so I don't have much competition. I probably don't have any right to think of myself as a writer yet—but I do. Being a writer, or even wanting to be one, requires stuff that most normal kids don't do that much. For instance, when you're a writer, you have to take lots of long walks in the woods. I know that sounds pretty lame and self-conscious, I totally admit it, but it's true. I'd feel like a complete phony saying it if I didn't actually enjoy doing it once in a while, taking time to myself, letting ideas for stories or poems just roll through my brain as I ignore the rest of the world.

Mr. Sensitive, huh? What bull.

If I'm being honest, I have to confess that I almost never write any stories or poems after these walks. Heck, I don't even take the walks very often. Whatever. I doubt that very many great writers did all that much walking in the woods anyway. At least not after the invention of TV, video games, and text messaging.

I know that Coleman Hardt sure isn't the kind of guy who walks around in the trees thinking, 'oh little bird, oh pretty little sucker of Siren tears,' and crud like that.

Okay, total truth time. I've actually only gone out by myself and walked around in the woods a few times as part of my writer's training. Most times, I've gone with girls who I'm trying to impress and who I hope will think I'm this real sensitive poet guy because I take these walks. I'm such a phony sometimes.

Why am I even thinking about this garbage right now? I must have bumped my head in the crash. What does walking in the woods have to do with lying here at the edge of a dark forest, hurting like hell next to an unconscious guy I barely know, both of us trapped? Maybe it's that I'm glad that I've at least spent some time in the wilderness before. It makes me a little less scared.

I stare out into the darkness, at all the black trees staring back at me and . . . crap . . . "a little less scared?" Definitely put the emphasis on "*a little.*" Better yet, put the emphasis on "*scared!*"

Speaking of things to be afraid of, I realize that there isn't any gas smell. My dad's 'vette is an amazing machine—I guess I should say *was* an amazing machine. The fuel injection probably cut off the gas the second we turned upside down. In movies, whenever a car crashes, there's usually a big explosion and fire ball. That kind of stuff looks great on the big screen, but without the slightest scent of gas in the air, I think that the odds of us blowing up are pretty low. But blowing up is far from my only worry.

Think, think, think! What exactly do I need to worry about out here?

Okay, I know that there are animals. What if there are wild beasts nearby? Mountain lions or hungry bears? They probably couldn't get in to hurt us any more than we can get out to escape from them. Still, I feel like a piece of meat, or a worm wriggling on a fishing hook—just waiting here trapped and helpless.

Why am I *trying* to think of things to be scared of? I should think of something positive. Think!

Okay, when we get out of this, I'll have a great story to write. It'll be one of those true stories, like an episode of *I Survived* or *I Shouldn't Be Alive* that nobody would ever believe if it was just made up. But because this story is true, people will be amazed. Maybe thinking more positively will help in this situation, though I doubt it. My body hurts a ton, but it's my ego that feels the most beat up. Has anybody in the history of the world ever been as big of a loser as I feel like right now?

You know how sometimes you can be doing great, really on top of your game, and you walk in someplace and some jerk says something cutting or stupid? Even though you pretend that it doesn't bother you, it totally screws up your mood. I heard an extreme pothead girl, Sierra Eggers, say to a jock who was teasing her about her purple Mohawk haircut, "You're harshing my mellow, dude." I thought it was one of the dorkiest things I'd ever heard, but I have to admit, I get what Sierra meant. My mellow is soooooo totally harshed right now.

I stare again at Coleman Hardt, my idol, my hero, the person I most admire in the world. Even in this dim light I can see his face, rugged and tough looking. It's not movie star good looks that make him so striking. In fact, seeing him up close, you can tell that his face has a lot of scars. You'd sure never call him pretty.

But he is the most famous person I've ever met. He's

been in every major magazine—*Time, Newsweek, People*—all of them. His photo, taken by a famous photographer, was once on the cover of *Interview Magazine* and is included in her book of portraits of painters, actors, poets, and authors like Cole.

No, not like Cole. No one is like Cole.

He has a large head and thick, spiked-up hair. His hands are surprisingly small. His white and blue striped shirt might once have been nice, but now it has cigarette burns just below the chest pocket. I noticed them earlier tonight at the reading, even though I was twenty rows back. Hardt is a shade below six feet tall, but unlike some men who look taller at that height than they really are, he looks shorter. I think it's his stockiness. He's leaning toward getting fat.

Am I allowed to say that, even to myself? Allowed to call him *fat?* I mean, it's kind of cruel and insulting in a way, right? Okay, screw that, this is *not* the time to have a debate with the P.C. side of myself. We're trapped in a crushed sports car in the damned forest. Hardt is not fat, but he's stocky. And staring at him now, which I can do because he's unconscious, I guess he is what you'd call ruggedly handsome. His success with the ladies is well-known, as are the tall tales of his drinking. That success with females is one of the things I'd wanted to ask him about . . . you know . . . before I may have accidentally . . . uh . . . *killed* him!

There are tiny pieces of broken windshield glass in his hair. I don't think you'd call them slivers because they're more like chunks. I lean over and look more carefully at his leg. I can see the piece of bone sticking up through his torn pant leg. It looks like a broken limb off a white birch tree. It's not a huge bone. I reach over and gently touch the area around the bone. His pant leg feels damp. When I look at my fingertips, I can see dark liquid. The dampness is his blood. I start to gag but close my eyes and breathe quick shallow breaths. If I were to throw up right now, I can't even imagine how bad that would feel to my ribs and shoulder.

God, don't let him die . . . Let him be okay . . .

Reality check: neither of us are 'okay.' We're lying here injured, me still belted-in upside down in my dad's totaled Corvette.

Yep, I'm so screwed I can't even find words for it.

All I can do is lie here very still, not moving at all. When I do this, my body doesn't hurt too bad—but my slightest movement just about kills me. All I can do right now is not move and try to control my thoughts, which is impossible.

Of all the kids at Spokane Falls Community College who wanted this simple task but great honor— *"One student will be selected to drive Mr. Hardt to the after-reading soiree at the Templeton's house on the back side of Mount Spokane"*—I got picked. Yep, I got the call.

I'm only 17 years old and not even a real college student yet. I'm in Running Start, a program for high school kids who want to get a head start on their college classes. When I had the chance to join Running Start, I jumped at it.

For a guy who wants to be a writer, hell for anybody over the age of 14, high school is useless. Think about it, football games (rah-rah-shish-boom-bah), dances (Me: Hi, wanna dance? Her: No, leave me alone), clubs (Chess? Science? Jesus? Bowling?), proms (Where do I even start?). Plus, most high school classes are lame: Contemporary World Problems, Math, PE. They actually made us study square dancing in PE . . . *square dancing*! I won't even start about hall passes and after school detention.

Let's face it, high school is a prison with fewer armed guards and a slightly smaller number of weightlifters with shaved heads and too many tattoos—but a prison nonetheless. When I got the chance to escape high school and go to college, I was all over it. Knowing already that I wanted to be a famous writer, I managed to become the poetry editor of the Community College Literary Magazine. And because of this, I was able to beg, plead, and manipulate my way into this chauffeur's job. I never used to understand what my dad meant when I heard him say, "Be careful what you wish for," but I sure get it now.

Reality check number 2: Before this opportunity to drive Cole Hardt to the party after his reading, and before

I crashed my dad's beloved Corvette, I was once upon a time—like a few hours ago—a fairly normal guy. I spent about half of every day thinking about girls—the other half was for sleeping, eating, and calling or text messaging my friends on my phone. I'm a Sagittarius but I don't really believe in astrology. I eat the same junk that every other kid I know eats, with a special addictive relationship to cheeseburgers. Hell, how much more typical could I be? Maybe I have a tiny bit more desire (or desperate need?) to achieve fame and fortune than most of my peers. But I know that a lot of them, if they are being honest, want it just as much as I do.

I had hoped that meeting Cole might somehow help me achieve my dream, but staring over at him now fills my eyes with tears. Killing Coleman Hardt is not exactly what I had in mind for this fame quotient of my goals. How selfish is that?

Cole is a big part of the reason I decided to be a writer in the first place. The primary reason I chose this goal is that without being famous, without getting some recognition from the world . . . how do I say this? Just straight out I guess. Without being known and making my mark, I think I'll always feel like I'm nothing. Less than nothing even— like I'm worm-crap, snail-slime, navel-lint, toe-jam. I know that none of these put-downs is particularly original. A real writer would be able to come up with his own collection of perfectly witty and unique images with which to slam himself, but you get my point. Clichés or not, unless I'm somebody, I'm nobody.

There are rich kids in our school driving Lexuses and Acuras who will someday inherit their daddy's businesses and wealth. There are jocks with varying degrees of talent, some loaded with it, and some just support players. But even the guys who are less talented are at least part of their teams. Despite my dad's one obvious indulgence—his Corvette—my family doesn't have all that much money. And I peaked athletically when I was, like, 12. So, I had to search out more options for becoming someone important in life.

Except for the actual drudgery and frustration of the writing part, prepping to become a famous writer is pretty easy. I have long hair and I dress very intentionally like I don't care how I look. I carry a moleskin notebook with me everywhere I go just in case the mood strikes me to write. That mood seems to arrive almost exclusively when I'm within eyeball shot of some cute girl who I hope will look at me, see my long, gorgeous hair, and think I'm interesting and deep because I'm a writing down my brilliant observations.

Total crap.

I may be the phoniest jerk-wad in the history of the universe! And that selfish thought of a few moments ago, what Cole said about me killing Hardt is probably right—that's probably the only thing I'll ever be famous for. Here's another even more selfish notion: something you may have noticed I keep thinking about over and over and over again . . .

I'm sooooo screwed!

Although the forest is dark, there's a three-quarter moon over our heads shedding enough light for me to see fairly well. It's mid-September, and we've had an Indian summer this year, long days and warm nights. I'm not sure what the weather forecast was for tonight, but so far it's not too cold. It's probably around 9 o'clock right now. I wonder, though, how cold it'll be later.

This land is either National or State Forest. I'm not really sure, but there are no houses for miles in any direction. The road is called a highway, but it's a two-lane blacktop, with lots of speed limit and winding road signs warning you to take it easy. As I lie here trapped and hurting, I realize that if I'd intentionally set out to find a more horrible place for this crash to happen, if I'd studied for weeks or months—hell, for years—I couldn't have picked a worse spot. You know when you're a total screw-up, right? I mean, it's obvious to you and obvious to everyone else. I know this kind of thinking isn't going to help us, but that doesn't mean I can stop thinking it. I feel totally stupid and ashamed. I wish I'd just hurry up and friggin' die.

The darkness of the forest is spooky. Through the spaces where the windows used to be I can see the first line of trees, tall black columns, impossible to ignore. Behind those trees, nothing good—more trees, animals, and miles of impenetrable darkness. I force myself to try and think about other things, stay in the present, and not panic, no matter how afraid I am.

Not everybody in America even knows the name Coleman Hardt. Serious writers and poets, and any English teacher you'd ever want to take a class from know him, but he's much more famous in Europe—especially in Germany, where he was born and lived until he was about 3. He's also very famous in France where he got drunk on a popular live TV show about literature called *Ellipses*. I've seen a tape of the show and on it he was drinking wine, a lot of wine. He got really drunk and started grabbing this other poet-woman's legs and insulting the snooty French host until finally Cole just tore off his own mic and walked off in the middle of the program. The snooty host about had a stroke, but the French public loved it. The incident made Cole Hardt a household name across all of Europe—the wild American artiste who didn't give a rip what anybody thought of him.

I wish he'd wake up again, but he looks pretty peaceful and comfortable for a guy who is lying in a wrecked sports car with a sharp, white knife of bone sticking up through his left pant leg. Looking at his face again, a face I've seen so many times in photographs and in articles online about him, I think about how much I admire him. Why do I feel this for a guy who spends a fair amount of time drunk and acting crazy?

I discovered his writing just last year in my Intro to Lit Class when our 11th grade English teacher, Mr. James, started the poetry unit.

Poetry.

I know, garbage, huh?

I'd never considered myself a poet, and never even thought about wanting to be one until that poetry class with Mr. James. I'd written some funny stories that kids in my English class had said were good, so I was already deciding that I wanted to be a writer. But as for poetry, I couldn't see how that had anything to do with my goals of wealth and fame.

In 10th grade, all the poems we read had that 'poet-y' sound to them, and they were meaningless to me. To be honest, most of them I couldn't even understand and still can't.

So last year, in 11th grade, when Mr. James stood up in front of our English class and said, "We'll start our study of poetry with my favorite history poem," I wasn't the only kid to groan.

But Mr. James just smiled. "This poem, by Coleman Hardt, is titled, *Uncle Walt*."

None of us had ever heard of Coleman Hardt, but everyone in class groaned or sighed. *Uncle Walt*? A history poem? Boorrrrriiiinnngggg! But Mr. James didn't miss a beat.

"My favorite history poem," he said once again. He repeated the title and then he read the poem aloud:

> *Honestly,*
> *How many of us*
> *Have ever read*
> *LEAVES OF GRASS*
> *Cover to cover?*
> *Or even half of it?*
> *How many know*
> *That the 1st edition was only*
> *80 pages or so,*
> *But that it grew*
> *To over 300*
> *During Uncle Walt's*
> *Long life?*

I think most of the kids in class knew that *Leaves of Grass* was written by Walt Whitman, an old-time dead guy who looked like the first hippie ever. Even I had heard of him.

> *Whitman is the great-grandfather*
> *Of American poetry.*
> *But I like to think of him*
> *Walking the streets of D.C.*
> *During the Civil War*
> *Heading to and from*
> *The military hospital*
> *Where he held the hands*
> *Of dying boys, taking down the words*
> *For their final*
> *Letters home.*
> *I think of Uncle Walt,*
> *As those boys called him*
> *And called out to him,*
> *Weeping quietly,*
> *Out of their presence, of course—*
> *But always going back,*
> *A freshly laundered shirt,*
> *His beard trimmed neatly*
> *Always back to them,*
> *Hour after hour,*

Day after day,
Loving them, caring for and about
All those dying boys
So many of them,
But each one precious.
Each face belonging to a single soul,
Touched and touching Walt
Until finally his nerves shattered,
His heart broke and
He could barely breathe.
But up until that very moment,
Think of him
At the end of each horrific day,
Walking home
Weeping again,
For all the pain and loss,
Then rising the next morning
To do it all once more.

It was weird. I felt a lump in my throat and a tingling as I saw the picture the poem drew, the dying, young soldiers, many no older than me, the pain that Whitman felt and his courage . . . then Mr. James read on . . .

Many mornings
On his way to this perdition

He'd pass by
Abraham Lincoln
Taking his own lonely journey,
Going, perhaps,
To the telegraph station,
The last place he'd been
The night before,
To collect his own latest
News of death and loss.
I think of
These two men
Making eye contact
And each nodding
Silently,
Maybe touching with fingertips
The brims of their hats
And going on.

By now the poem had me totally in its grip. I'd never thought of Lincoln or Whitman as real people, as human beings torn apart by the sadness they were living through . . .

Walt would later write about
The pain in Lincoln's face,
Especially in his eyes,
And about the

Humanity of the man,
Flesh and blood,
Sinew and spirit, rocked
To the deepest darkness
A man can know—
Lincoln,
Not yet marble and iconic,
Walt himself
Not realizing
His own coming immortality
On the bookshelves of
Millions.
This was
Before all that.
This was back when
They walked
Quietly
Towards and past one another,
Carrying burdens of unimaginable
Weight,
In shared and separate
Duties,
Day after day,
Week after week—
In truth,
For all eternity.

When Mr. James finished reading, he closed the book and smiled at us but didn't say anything for maybe half a minute or longer. The feeling in the room was one of respect and maybe even awe at what we'd just heard. Keats and Shakespeare and old dead John Donne exploded in my head into a million little pieces of cast-off brain cell fluff. The whole class, all of us, just sat there, pin-drop silent.

Mr. James finally said, "If that's not a great history poem, I don't know what is. What do you think?"

I didn't raise my hand or even listen to the suck-up kids who always answer all the in-class questions, but I realized that, for the first time in my life, I totally understood what a poem meant. I got why Mr. James called it a "history poem" too. He was tricking us. And the message was so clear. History is not just about famous battles and great empires. It's about the people who once lived and walked right where we're walking and living today. It's about what they felt for another, and the poem meant something even more to me. It made me think about writing, and about using words so perfectly that something impossible happens—good writing, great writing could deeply touch our hearts and change us.

By the end of that school day, I had read that poem a dozen times because I loved it so much.

After school that night, when I got back home, I dropped my backpack onto my bed and went straight to my computer. I googled Coleman Hardt and found out everything I could about him. Well, I should say that I *started* to find out. It turned out there were 2,367,000 hits on the Google search for Coleman Hardt. I've been reading about him, and reading his poems, stories and novels, ever since. From that day forward, I knew that if I could ever write poems the way Cole Hardt did, I wanted to be a poet too. To be totally honest, that poem made me realize, for the first time ever, that being a writer—a great one like Hardt—could do something more than just make a guy famous. It could change the way you look at things, maybe even change your life.

Right now, thinking about school, about poetry and Cole and all that stuff, it seems almost like none of it ever happened, none of it feels real. I reach down with my right hand, and even this small gesture creates sharp stabbing pains through the whole left side of my body. I touch the inside of the roof, which is below me now, and feel the smooth texture of the hard plastic. I have to make myself think about other things, NOT the terror I feel every time I look out at the woods . . .

Meeting Cole Hardt in person, I realize how little I really did know him. In some ways he seems to be a lot like everything I've read or heard about him. He drinks and talks and acts a little like a wild, younger guy. As near as I can tell, he's not afraid of anybody or anything, especially when he's been drinking, which he was doing before and during his reading tonight.

In all the biographies about him, they tell how when he was 25-years-old, he drank himself into an exploding ulcer and ended up in the charity ward of a big Los Angeles hospital. A doctor told him that if he ever touched another drink, he'd be dead within a week. When he was released, that very night he mixed some milk in with his beer and he's been drinking ever since. He is the first to admit that he's an alcoholic and that he has no intention of ever quitting.

Okay, I'm not saying that I think Cole's drinking is cool, or that he's a saint. But Cole Hardt is the guy who made me want to be a poet like him, by teaching me the power of great writing.

Of course, back when I first discovered Cole, I had no idea that within a year, we'd be trapped together in my dad's wrecked Corvette. I didn't know that I would be the person responsible for our situation.

Damn!

I'm thirsty. My mouth feels super dry. Of course, we have no water, no food, nothing here with us in what's left of the car. After all, this ride was supposed to take about forty-five minutes.

I'm sure everyone heading to the party thought Cole and I would take the I-90 freeway east to the Rathdrum exit, then to Rathdrum and west again at Highway 54, as that's the fastest way to get to the Templeton's place. That's the route on the map that they handed out. If anyone is looking for us, or I should say, when they start to look, that's where they will be looking. No one will think to look way out here in the boonies. Most people don't even know about this back way to Rathdrum. I do because this is the way my parents and I always go to our lake place, but nobody knew we were going this way. I didn't know myself until a few seconds before I decided.

I'd give anything to have not made this choice. The freeway isn't perfectly safe, but there are rarely any deer loping into your path. And if you do crash on the freeway, other cars will see you and come help.

Why the hell did I come this isolated, lonely, dangerous back way? How did it happen?

When Cole Hardt and I finally got to the car after the reading, I asked him if he'd like to take a shortcut to the party.

Without looking at me, he'd said, "nice car," and then climbed in, grunting and mumbling about how awkward and difficult it was to get into the leather bucket seat that was only about eight inches above the pavement. I wasn't sure he'd heard my question about the shortcut because he just stared out the front window. And before I could ask him again, he said, "What I'd like to do is go back to my hotel and get drunk. Since that's not an option, the quicker you can get me there, and *out of there*, the better."

"Okay."

"What's your name again?" he asked. We'd been introduced quickly in the middle of a crowd of autograph seekers right after his big reading in the Spartan Theatre, so I wasn't surprised that he didn't remember. But before I could answer, he said, "Ryan, right?"

I couldn't stop smiling. "Ryan Turane. Yes, sir."

"Cut the Mr. and Sir crap, okay? I'm Cole, you're Ryan, and any time either of us takes a dump, it smells bad."

I laughed.

Cole, pretending to be serious, asked, "Your shit *does* stink doesn't it?"

"Oh, yeah," I answered.

He smiled. "Good. Everybody's does, but some people think theirs doesn't. I'm glad you're not one of them."

There were a million things I wanted to say to him, ten million questions I wanted to ask as we drove. When did you start writing and why? When did you know you would be great? Do you listen to music when you write? What kind? How many women have you slept with thanks to being famous? How do you meet them? Have you met many movie stars? What kind of house do you live in now—a mansion? What kind of car do you drive—a Ferrari? Do the paparazzi bug you much?

But I wasn't sure how to start asking things until he said to me, "So, you like my work, huh?"

"I love it," I answered. "You're the best writer in the world."

What had I said? Could I possibly sound like a bigger suck-up? I turned about two hundred degrees of red-faced, but it was how I really felt. Besides, there was no hope of my being totally Mr. Cool with him anyway—after all, he was my idol.

Cole smiled a little and asked, "How old are you, Ryan?"

"Seventeen."

"How'd you get picked to drive me tonight?"

I explained about the college's literary magazine, *Iron Debacles,* and told him that I'm the poetry editor.

Cole laughed. "So, I owe you for accepting my poems?"

I laughed too. "Heck, you're Cole Hardt. Nobody in their right mind would reject your work."

"Is that right? Then how come I've got a big trunk full of rejection slips, some of them from as recently as last week?"

"No!"

"Oh, yeah," he said. "Sometimes editors reject me just to say they did, sometimes because they already have all the poems they need for their next issue, and sometimes, probably, because the particular poems I send to them stink."

"Bull," I blurted out, surprising myself before quickly adding, "Sorry, but I don't believe that. You're famous and your poems are amazing. You're a genius."

Hardt laughed and gave a great snort that made some nasty looking stuff fly out of his nose. He wiped it off with the back of his hand, totally unselfconscious and unembarrassed, then wiped that on his pant leg. "If you're gonna say idiotic things, warn me first, alright?"

"Sorry," I said, blushing again and ignoring the goober disaster of a few seconds before. "I'm just surprised that anybody would reject your work."

"Naaaa," Cole said. "Being a writer, especially a poet, your life is one of constant rejection. I sent a lot of poems and stories out for a long time before I started getting published much."

I was nervous to try and visit with Cole. If you've ever read his writing, even a small sample, you'd know that he isn't very social. Over and over again, interviewers and biographers say that he doesn't like most people and hates to talk about himself. So, I was nervous trying to visit with him. After all, I was just the dumb kid who was assigned to drive him. I knew I should shut up, but how many times was I going to get to talk to Cole Hardt, sit with him—just the two of us—and pick his brain? Plus, I hadn't expected him to be friendly and to talk so openly with me. Since he was willing, I kept at it, figuring that our time alone in the car would be brief and my only chance to talk with him.

"What's it like to be famous?" I asked.

He looked back at me and let out a long breath, more like a sigh, as though the question really bored him. Finally, he said, "Famous? There's no such thing."

"What do you mean? You've been in all these magazines and on TV. They've made movies out of your books. That's fame isn't it?"

He said, "Most of what people call fame is actually just celebrity crap. You know what a celebrity is, Ryan?"

I tried to impress him by repeating something I'd read once in an essay. "Sure," I said, like the know-it-all I can sometimes be, "A celebrity is somebody who is so famous that he can totally trash a five-star hotel room and still be invited back."

Cole smiled, "Yeah, there's a little of that I suppose, but celebrity is mostly about turning a person into an object, a thing used to make money by selling an image, which may or may not—usually does *not*—have anything to do with who that person really is. There's a whole industry out there—newspapers, magazines, the internet, and TV shows dedicated to selling celebrities and helping people create fantasies that someday they'll be a celebrity too. It's all bullshit."

"Well, why do you write then if you don't want to be famous?"

Cole laughed. "Writing and striving for fame have nothing to do with each other. Fame and celebrity are turds in your soup bowl, crap that you eventually have to eat in order to get paid for writing. The turds are not your goal. They are nasty, side-feces, and unless you remember that fame is mostly about eating crap, those turds can kill you."

I tried to think about what he was saying, tried to understand it, but it didn't seem right to me. I mean, the main reason I want to be a writer is so that I can get famous and everyone will know me, and I'll have all this power. That may be kind of lame or pathetic or shallow, but it's true.

"You honestly don't care about being famous, being loved, and having your writing change people's lives?" I asked.

"I care about my writing," Cole said, looking straight ahead at the trees and farm fields through which we were passing. "I care about being honest about my life. If that honesty resonates with some people, that's fine. But I don't especially care about my readers, strangers, the downtrodden masses. I don't write to save mankind. I write to save myself."

But I still couldn't let go of this fame thing. It's always been the biggest part for me—more than getting rich, more than anything else—to be famous and have people want to know me and love my writing and love me for writing it, and also like the way I felt towards Cole's history poem. Even if my dad acts like he doesn't like me most of the time, and even if hardly anybody gives a crap whether I'm alive or not, my great hope has been that being a famous author will someday change all of that.

"But if you weren't famous," I said, "then nobody would ever see your writing, would they?"

"That'd be okay with me. I spent a lot of years writing stuff that nobody ever saw."

We cruised into a long, looping curve in the road, and I gave the Corvette a little bit more gas so that I could show off its great handling. Cole didn't seem to notice the surge in power. He seemed to still be thinking about my last question.

"I put up with a certain amount of 'fame' to keep from having to work crap jobs to survive. You write for yourself, Ryan, and if your work gets out there and people find it and you get paid for it, great, that's all good. But Emily Dickinson wrote hundreds of poems and never published a single one under her own name in her lifetime. After she died, they found seventeen little notebooks stuffed with all her poems neatly printed. Now she's as immortal as a person can get, but she wasn't ever famous. Today she'd be branded a loser."

When Cole said this thing about being a loser, I recalled one of his poems. "You remember that poem you wrote about losing but always doing the same stuff just the same?"

Cole smiled. He paused a moment, closed his eyes like he was concentrating and then, from memory, recited:

Unable…
…to handle the pain
and grief
of losing.

I do what most
people
do in this situation.
I pursue,
with vigor and
total commitment
a new opportunity
to feel it again!

Fuckin' humans!

I laughed out loud, just like I did the first time I'd ever read that poem. I love that little surprise line at the end. I was also amazed. Cole has published close to five hundred poems in fifteen books. How could he recite one just from memory?

"Do you memorize every poem you've written?" I asked.

"Oh, hell no," Cole said. "But some of them I remember." He paused then asked, smiling again, "Why would a guy memorize what he writes? Isn't the purpose of writing to get the thing down so that you *don't* have to memorize it?"

I blushed again, but I wanted to get back on the subject. "If immortality is so boring, what difference did Emily Dickinson's poems make anyway?"

I was thinking about Yeats and Shakespeare again, their 'immortal' poems that I hated.

Cole didn't hesitate. "I don't care about her poems. I don't even like most of 'em. What I love is that she got to write them, she got to live her life as a poet. Fame and celebrity had nothing to do with it. Old Emily got to run the greatest game of all, spend her life with the words, working with them, loving them, massaging them, and being massaged by them in return. She's been dead for a hundred years, but if you're lucky enough to spend all your time on earth writing, like she did, death doesn't matter much because you've already experienced heaven."

So 'heaven' to Coleman Hardt wasn't the fame, but just the writing itself? I knew that it wasn't the same for me. As we drove along in silence, I realized that I didn't even like to write that much. I do it because it's the only thing I'm a little bit good at, but lots of times it's boring. I know that this is a bad sign for a guy who wants to be a famous author. But sitting in a room, just writing, putting down the words of a poem or story . . . I mean, I do it because I have to if I'm ever going to get famous and be known by people and loved and have strangers ask for my autograph. I do it because I want really cool people, and especially gorgeous girls like movie stars and supermodels, to want to hang out with me. What good is being famous if you don't take advantage of it, if you don't use fame to make gorgeous girls hot for you. (Hello, Gabrielle Reid, the most amazing girl alive . . . can you hear me now?) Why be famous if you can't make guys jealous, and the whole world wish they were you? But the actual writing itself? I dunno. After our conversation, I knew that I was no Cole Hardt—not yet anyway. And who was I kidding? I knew I probably never would be.

I try to take a deep breath and pain shoots through my left side again. I look out at the black trees, look at the hood of the car—it's amazing how smooth it looks, like it's not even dented or cracked. I'm dented and cracked pretty bad and Cole worse than me. Writing? Fame? Even though those thoughts are still running through my brain, the darkness, the pain, the scary dangerousness of my situation is swallowing me every chance it gets, making me ashamed and stupid and feeling as helpless as I actually am.

Damn, this is nasty. I don't know what to do.

Cole wakes up again, turns to me, and asks, "How you doin' kid?"

"I'm so sorry," I say.

"Why?"

"You're injured, and we're in this mess. It's all my fault."

"Wasn't your fault at all," Cole says, his voice calm. "It was us or the deer, and if you'd hit him, I'd probably have a damned antler sticking through my chest right now."

Cole saying this makes me remember the accident, how we got here. I swear to God, I was going the speed limit, only 45. We rounded a curve, and I was watching the road, paying close attention, and driving carefully, when a big buck, a whitetail deer with a huge rack of antlers, ran right in front of us from the thick bushes on our right. When he saw our headlights, he froze. I swerved hard to miss him. The left-front tire of the car caught the gravel, and we started to slide. I over-corrected, and in half a heartbeat, we were sliding sideways, and that left-front tire was in the gravel on *our* side of the road.

Suddenly we were upside down and airborne. I'm not sure what happened next because once we were in the air, I closed my eyes and just gripped the steering wheel as tightly as I could.

When we stopped moving, I opened my eyes again. The car was upside down, way off the side of the road. For some reason, neither of our airbags deployed, probably because we never really hit anything but the ground. Regardless of how this accident happened, the fact is I've got to think of something I can do to get us help. But I don't have a clue what that might be. I'm not exactly a master problem-solver. Hell, I can't even pass Geometry—no, I mean I *really* can't pass it. I had it last year in 11th grade and flunked it. So, I went to summer school and took it there too, and I flunked it again! Fortunately, all my other grades are good, mostly A's, so I made it into Running Start. Right about now I almost wish I hadn't—if I hadn't been at the college, Cole and I wouldn't be in this mess right now.

"I'm sorry anyway," I say. "I'm such an idiot . . ."

Cole interrupts, "You need to try and take it easy, Ryan. We're stuck here until somebody spots us. We just have to relax, maybe visit a little bit. That's the best thing we can do. No point beating yourself up. No situation is so bad that it can't be made worse by having a negative, crappy attitude, right?"

"Yeah, I guess."

But the truth is that even as he speaks, Cole's voice sounds like he's in pain—not scared but hurting. And speaking of hurting, I'm feeling worse and worse too.

How the hell am I going to save us? There must be something I can do to get us out of this jam . . .

7

My cell phone! I swear to God, I'm brain dead. Why
didn't I think of it before?

I look over at Cole. "I've got my cell phone."

He glances back at me and says, "I can't stand those
things."

"What?"

"Cell phones . . . they're the most annoying invention of
all time. Every asshole in the world thinks his conversations
are fascinating to anybody within a fifty-yard radius."

"But I can call for help."

Cole just says, "Okay."

I squirm around slowly, each movement hurting like
crazy, until I manage to get my right hand into my right-
front pocket of my jeans and, carefully as I can, slide the
phone out with two fingers. Every move I make, even the
slightest shifting of my weight, makes my back spasm with
sharp pains, like a knife is sticking me over and over again.

My left shoulder hurts too, but I manage to fight through the pain and slowly twist the phone in my hand until I have a good grip on it. If I drop this phone, I don't know how I'll be able to pick it up again. I hurt too much.

I reach across my body with my left hand, pain shooting down my back and across my shoulder. Now I cradle the phone in both hands and turn on the power button.

Cole stares at me.

It takes a few moments for the phone to come on, but when it finally does, it says, *Searching for Signal.* This is not a good sign. I keep staring at the little screen. *Searching for signal . . . searching for signal . . . No signal available, try again later . . . searching for signal . . .*

"How we doing?" Cole asks.

"We're okay," I say, putting my index finger on the top of the phone to try and use my body as an extra antenna. I move the phone up and down, one side to the other, slowly, quickly, circling one direction then back the other way. Every move is killing me, but I keep trying to find a signal.

After several minutes, I still have nothing.

Cole asks, "No reception?"

"No, I can't get a signal here. At least not yet."

Even in the darkness I can see Cole smile. In a low and calm voice, he says, "Like I said, I hate cell phones."

8

We've been quiet for a while now, I'm not sure how long.
Even though I'm wearing my watch, it hurts when I turn
my arm to try and check the time, and in the darkness, I
can't see it anyway.

I feel so ashamed and embarrassed. I keep trying to
control my emotions but it's hard. My whole left side hurts
so badly, and Cole is injured worse than me. What a jerk
I am . . .

I have to get my mind straight, have to stop being so
negative. Thinking about our predicament, I finally turn to
Cole and say, "I can't sit upside down any longer."

Cole says, "Okay, you gonna unbuckle and get down so
you can sit upright?"

"I'm gonna try."

"I'll help you then," Cole says. He reaches across and
puts one hand on my head and grabs my right arm with
his other hand. He squeezes my right arm pretty hard,

getting a good grip. For half a second, I think how cool it is that Cole Hardt has his hands on me, trying to help me. I mean, it's just like we're the same, two guys in a jam trying our best to support each other—literally in this case.

I know that to move my body this much is going to hurt a lot, but I have to do it. I place my right hand down onto the roof of the car, which is below me. Being smashed in as badly as it is, it isn't that far down.

Cole says, "Tell me when you're ready."

"I'm ready now. Here goes . . ." I take as deep a breath as I can and reach over and unbuckle my seatbelt.

The second I start to slide down, pain rips through me, the worst pain I've ever felt, a blinding, paralyzing pain . . . I hear myself cry out . . . everything goes black and now a sharp flash of white and I'm floating . . . and I feel nothing . . .

As if coming from a million miles away, I hear a faint voice, "Ryan . . . Ryan . . ." calling out to me. Who is it? My dad? God? The devil? I open my eyes, and for a few seconds I have no idea where I am.

"Ryan . . . easy does it, buddy . . ."

I look towards the voice and see the face of Cole Hardt . . . what's he doing here?

"Ryan," he says again.

"Yeah," I say. "Am I okay?"

"Sure," Cole says. "You just passed out for a couple seconds."

"I did?"

And now I remember everything. I am sitting upright on the inside of the Corvette, leaning back. My shoulders are propping me up against the console, where the stereo buttons are. My legs are stretched out, one on top of the other, in the space between the bucket seats.

I ask, "How did I get sitting like this?"

"I took advantage of your little nap to move you around and get you into what looked like the best position."

Once again, I feel a bad throbbing in my shoulder and pain in my back and all along the left side of my body. I try to clear my throat and another bolt of white pain slams me. Tears come to my eyes, but I hold them in.

"Thanks, Cole. I feel okay."

He smiles. "Sure, you do."

I take steady, slow, shallow breaths, concentrating as hard as I can to not think about my pain. Slowly and carefully, I move my right hand, lifting it to my left shoulder. There is a huge bump, pressing tightly against the skin.

"Ahhhh," I moan. "I think my left shoulder is out of the socket."

Cole reaches across and gently feels the bump. "No, that's your clavicle, for sure. Half of the bone is sitting on top of the other half. Pretty painful huh?"

"Yeah," I say. "But my whole left side hurts worse than my shoulder."

"Ribs," Cole says. "Once you break those—hell, even bruise 'em—you're going to feel it for a while."

I get what he means. I can't even breathe without pain, a lot of pain.

We are quiet again. I can hear him breathing, low and steady. I feel my own breathing too, coming in short gasps. When I try to take a deeper breath, the pain comes back.

Finally, I say, "Should we move you into a more comfortable position too?"

"No," Cole says. "I'm worried about this bone moving around too much. If it was sharp enough to pierce my skin and my pant leg, I don't want it slicing into my femoral. Besides, let's give you some time to recover from your move before we try anything else."

"Okay," I answer.

"Is this Corvette your car?" he asks.

"No, my dad's."

"You're gonna be in some deep shit when you get home."

"Yeah, probably."

We stop talking again. In this silence, Cole closes his eyes and rests. Since he's not watching me, I try my cell phone again, waving it around to find a signal but with no luck.

I let Cole sleep. I stay quiet and just let my mind roam . . .

I think back to Dad letting me take the Corvette tonight, to our complex negotiation. My father doesn't hate me, I know that. But he doesn't like me either. I mean, I don't care what he thinks of me once I'm famous and everybody knows me and loves me—or at least looks up to me and admires me. Why should I care how my old man feels about me then? I don't think about that kind of thing very often, and for some reason, when I think it now it feels immature and stupid of me.

Dad was a Navy fighter pilot. He won the Air Medal and a bunch of other medals for flying combat missions during the Desert Storm War. I'm an only child and a late arrival at that. Dad is fifty-eight years old. To say we're not real close is a big understatement. But again, being in the situation that I'm in right now, I can't stop thinking about what he would say, what he'd do, and how much I trust him when I push aside all my teenage rebellion BS.

So far as I knew, my dad and mom hadn't ever taken much interest in my writing, which I figured was probably a good thing anyway, since lots of my stories are about this character named Artie Simon. I call him 'fat little rat-boy: Mommy's joy, Daddy's toy.' The theme of the stories is that Artie's dad doesn't understand him. Real original, huh? I am pretty amazingly lame-o sometimes. But that's the crap I've been writing—juvenile, self-pitying, idiotic garbage. My dad hasn't encouraged me to be a writer, but he hasn't ever tried to advise me against it either.

There is another thing I have to say about writing, though. While I always say that I want to be rich and famous, there are other parts of it too, like that poem from Cole about Walt Whitman and Lincoln, that I think are cool. Another thing that I haven't ever talked about, barely even thought about—a part that isn't shallow and full of crap. All my life I've been fascinated—almost hypnotized—by books.

I remember the first time I walked into my new best friend Brad Slater's house when we were about ten, the summer before fifth grade. I'd recently moved into a new neighborhood and Brad and I had met while hanging around the boring, suburban street in front of my house. He was kind of quiet and a little bit shy, but I was loud and silly and I started a conversation, asking him what there was "to do around here?" Stuff like that, anything to make a first friend. We ended up playing catch, throwing a baseball back and forth. He was much stronger and more athletic than I was, but I held my own.

He invited me back to his house for lunch. We hiked up the hill to his place and went in through the back door. I met his mom, who dressed very hot and sexy and looked like a beauty queen. She welcomed me, and I'd have probably never taken my eyes off her if Brad hadn't invited me into their family room to introduce me to his dad.

Mr. Slater had curly hair and was friendly, more relaxed and outgoing than Brad or Brad's mom, more like my personality actually. But what struck me most at the time was that Mr. Slater had his very own private library. Next to where he sat that day was a bookshelf, just like the bookshelves they had at school and in the school library and even in the public library where my mom took me sometimes when I was little. And on this bookshelf were a lot of books, more than a hundred. I'd never before seen a family with their very own library.

I asked, "Are those your books, Mr. Slater?"

He smiled at me. "Yes, whose books did you think they were?"

I wasn't sure how to answer, so I just mumbled the truth. "I didn't know normal people could have books, a bunch of books like this in their house, and own them just for themselves."

He looked at me kind of funny and said, "Well, you can purchase and own books if you want to. You can have as many of them as you like and can afford."

I was mesmerized by the rows of books, the colors of them—brown, black, blue and red—and by the writing on their edges. I tilted my head to the side so I could read the words.

Mr. Slater, noticing my interest said, "Titles, authors' names, and publishers."

I didn't know what he meant and looked at him confused, not even able to think how to ask what he was talking about.

He smiled and explained, "The writing on the sides of the books—actually they are called the spines—and the words on the spines are the titles of the books and the authors' name and, this little writing here," he pointed to one of the books with a blue spine, at the tiny gold writing on the bottom, "this is the publisher's name right here."

I looked at it and read it out loud, "Doubleday?"

"Yep," he said.

And that was the beginning of my love affair with books, starting before I had even much interest in reading, never mind writing. It seemed to me that even then, when I was pretty young, I knew that each of those books was a part of the person whose name was on the spine. They were people I'd never heard of before—Ernest Hemingway, James Dickey, Mario Puzo, Roland Smith—but each of them was right there in that house, at least their words and ideas were there, which was a big part of them. Whether the people who wrote the books were even still alive or not didn't matter, because the part of themselves they'd put into their books was still totally alive and that part of them would live forever. Even though I didn't know it at the time, that was the moment I decided to be a writer, way back when I was only ten. That's when I started to make the choice.

Speaking of choices, lying here hurting and scared, I realize that I've made some stupid choices that drive my dad crazy. Maybe the biggest of these is my hair. When Dad was young, there were guys like him who served their country in crew-cuts and preppy clothes and guys who . . . well . . . looked like me. Hippy types who had long hair and wore ratty-ass clothes and were against war and did protest marches and crap like that. My dad has never been real fond of the "hippy look" as he calls it. In fact, Dad shaves his head every morning. He has a mustache and a little goatee, but Mom makes him have them so that, as she puts it, "it won't look like he's going through chemo."

My hair is long and thick, flowing over the top of my shoulders. I'm also trying to grow a mustache, but let's just say that it is a work in minimal-progress. Most people don't seem to care that much about whether you have long hair or short. I mean, kids with different hair styles hang out with one another all the time, and you see people with long hair or short hair working together all over the place and nobody cares. But my dad is trapped in the conservative Republican version of the crew-cut 1970s. My hair drives him crazy. Truthfully, part of the reason I wear long hair is to bug him, I think.

After I was selected to chauffeur Cole Hardt, I approached my dad to ask about borrowing his car. Dad's Corvette is his baby. As a former fighter pilot, you have to know that he loves speed. He's had a Corvette for as long as I can remember. He bought this one six months ago, selling his 1976 Stingray so he could get a newer model. He's only let me drive this car a few times and he's been with me every time. He knows I can handle it, though, because we've gone out in it and he's watched me drive, both this newer Corvette and his older one. But getting him to let me take it by myself seemed pretty unlikely. I knew that Dad might consider it because my piece of crap, ten-thousand-year-old Buick Century breaks down fairly often and is pushing 220,000 miles (Okay, not 'ten-thousand-year-old', but eighteen, almost nineteen—hell, the car is older than me!) I hoped that Dad would understand that my car wasn't going to cut it as transportation for a celebrity.

There was no easy way to finesse the request, so I just hit it head on. "Dad, I get to drive my favorite writer in the world to this thing after his reading at the college and I want to use the Corvette."

Dad looked up from the newspaper and said, "You know the deal."

I knew he would say this. 'The deal' was simple. If I

would cut off my long hair, he'd let me borrow the car. We'd discussed this other times when I'd wanted to take the Corvette out, and this was his price tag.

"I can't do the haircut thing, Dad. Not before the party."

"Can't huh? Thousands of lives hang in the balance, do they?"

Dad can be pretty sarcastic when he wants to.

"No," I admitted. "But I want to feel my best for Cole Hardt's visit, and I feel my best with long hair."

"This Hardt guy is coming to Spokane?" I could hear the surprise in Dad's voice. "He's your boy, isn't he?"

Dad's surprise was no more than mine. I couldn't believe that Dad had even heard of Cole Hardt.

"How did you know that?" I asked.

"Call it my last-gasp effort at parental controls. I knew you were into him, so I checked him out a little bit."

I blushed, imagining Dad reading some of Cole's poems—the ones about sex and drugs and drinking, the one's with tons of profanity. I figured that any chance I might have for borrowing the car was over. But Dad surprised me.

"He's got some good stuff," he said.

I couldn't believe my ears, and Dad must have noticed my skepticism because he asked, "What? You don't believe I've read him?"

I didn't say anything.

Dad said, "Actually, I remember some of his poems pretty well. He wrote one titled, *Ah Yeah*, something like that, about loneliness and how there are a lot worse things than being lonely but that there's nothing worse than waiting too long to figure this out."

Although I couldn't remember which poem Dad might be talking about, it sure sounded like one of Cole's.

Dad continued, "Another one I liked was about women's lib. How maybe when women stop carrying little mirrors in their purses with them everywhere they go, they'll feel more liberated. He's a smart, funny guy."

"I know," I blurted out. "He's great."

Dad was quiet for a few seconds and then said, "He's a good writer. But I'm not sure how good a man he is."

I gave Dad a look, unintentional, but he picked up the vibe right away and backed off.

"That's not fair of me," Dad said. "I don't know him and so I have no idea what kind of man he is. Let's just say I made a lot of different choices than he did and leave it at that."

"Yes, sir," I answered.

Dad's military background gives him a great appreciation of manners, and when I really need something from him, I can totally turn it on like I'm some little gentleman. As I waited for Dad's next response, still surprised that he knew anything about Hardt, I thought for a moment how cool it would be to get to show off that I had a cool car.

Dad stared at me and finally said, "Sorry, Ryan, but Hardt or not, I have to stick to my guns. No haircut, no car."

I knew he would say this, so I was ready.

"This is what I'll do," I said, hating having to say it, but knowing that there was no way around it. "Before graduation this spring, before I walk and get my diploma, I'll get my hair cut any way you want me to. I promise you right now that if you'll let me use the car just this one time, I'll cut my hair."

My dad smiled and, totally surprising me and blowing my mind, he put out his hand for me to shake, which I did.

"Deal," he said.

I gulped hard and said, "deal" right back at him.

I'm pretty sure that totaling the Corvette was not included in our agreement. Hopefully, Dad will just consider it a minor amendment to our contract. If I'm gonna shave my head and look like him, wrecking the car seems like a fair trade.

"What's your father like?" Cole asks, interrupting my thoughts, bringing us right back to the conversation we were having before he dozed off, the thing about my borrowing the car.

"He's okay," I answer.

Cole pauses a second and now speaks in a voice low and sad, "My old man was a sadistic bully."

I knew this already from having read so much of Cole's work. He mentions his father in a number of his poems. But for him to say it to me now, to hear him speak about it and to see his face as he does, it seems a hundred times worse than just reading it. When you read the words, Cole sounds tough and strong and able to handle anything. But the hurt in his voice as he talks about it now, even all these years later, the sadness and pure sorrow, breaks your heart. I think about my dad and feel guilty that I haven't appreciated him more.

"Why was your dad so mean?" I ask.

"Why is anybody like they are? Why do some people dive onto hand grenades to save their buddies and other people kidnap five-year-old girls and rape them and then kill them? My old man was unhappy with his life, hated his job, hated my mother, who he also beat and who I hated for always just standing by and letting him beat me. He enjoyed seeing people in pain. He was just wired like that . . . couldn't help it."

I think about what Cole is saying and admit, "My dad's not like that. He's strict sometimes and he won't be too happy that I've totaled his car. But if we get out of this alive, he'll be glad that I'm okay."

Cole smiles. "*If* we get out of it alive, huh?"

"Sorry, not *if* . . . I didn't mean *if* . . . I meant *when*. W*hen* we get found and rescued."

Cole, still smiling, says, "I prefer *if*. Without a close call once in a while, like walking past an open twelfth story window, or sitting in a dark room, gun cocked, safety off, and that marvelous taste of steel from the barrel in your mouth—without teasing death every now and then—how can you ever fully appreciate whatever magic it is that keeps you from pulling the trigger?"

"Yeah, I know what you mean," I say.

Cole smiles, staring into my eyes. "You do, huh?"

I pause, think about how getting my hair cut in a few months is the most traumatic thing in my pampered life. And I think about Cole with the barrel of a gun in his mouth. How else would he know what that feels like unless he experienced it himself?

"No," I admit, trying not to think about that loaded gun. "No, to be honest, I don't know what you mean."

"That's good, Ryan. With any luck, you never will."

It's cold and dark and scary out here, and the longer
we're here the colder and darker and scarier it gets. You'd
think you'd get used to it, but I'm sure not. Forcing myself
to not look at the woods, to get my mind on something
else, I think about Cole's dad, his cruelty. And now I think
about when I was about thirteen years old, one day my dad
came out of the house as I was getting ready to put the lawn
mower away. He looked at the lawn, which I'd just finished
mowing as fast as I could so that I could go hang out with
my friends.

Dad said, softly but firmly, "You missed some spots."

"Where?" I asked, even though I could see that the yard
looked like it had gotten a bad haircut.

Dad ignored my question. "Mow it again, please."

"But I just mowed it," I whined.

Dad spoke, still no anger in his tone, but some obvious
disappointment. "Mow it again, properly this time."

Where we stood, behind the house, I stared at Dad. My hands were behind my back. I knew that my father couldn't see my hands and I was so pissed that I started giving him the finger. First just one hand, and then the other. I stuck my middle fingers up and silently screamed words to myself, cursing, imagining all the things I wished I could say but wouldn't. I was furious.

"Get to it," Dad said.

"Yes, sir," I answered, but I felt glad that I was flipping Dad off. In that moment, I hated him.

Dad walked past me into the house, and I grabbed the lawn mower and turned to start mowing again. And that's when I realized that the big basement picture window was right behind where I'd just been standing. Had Dad seen my obscene gestures in the reflection? I knew he must not have, or he would have said something, wouldn't he? In some ways, though, I didn't care if he had seen. I almost wished he had. I didn't like his control over me—what I saw back then as being mean.

That's not how I feel anymore. Being here in this shitty situation with Cole, and hearing him tell me about his dad's cruelty, I think I understand what my dad has been trying to do with me. What Dad has always tried to do is make me tougher, stronger, and better. Maybe my dad's strictness has made it possible to survive what's happening right now? That is, of course, *if* I—if *we*—survive.

In some way I can't explain, Cole and my dad seem to have a lot in common. It's nothing I can name exactly, but something in the way they look at the world and don't bend or break. Something in how honest they both are makes them alike. For the last year, I've wished that someone like Cole were my dad. For the first time now, I see that my dad is already a lot like the best parts of Cole.

My ribs and my shoulder feel worse the longer we are out here, even though it is better to be sitting upright. Everything I do—breathing, clearing my throat, trying to talk—it all hurts. But it hurts to not talk even more because Cole was right when he said that talking could help to take my mind off the pain.

When Cole talked about dying a few moments ago, the open window and the cocked gun, I shuddered, wondering when we'll be rescued, when someone will find us. But what will happen if they can't find us?

Cole seems to read my mind. "Don't worry about us dying out here, Ryan."

"Why not?"

"I'm not gonna die out here, after everything I've lived through. There's no way I'm getting off that easy."

"Easy?" I can't believe he thinks that this is 'easy.'

He speaks softly, "The guy who inspired me to write, who I looked up to and admired more than any other writer, was Jim Fantre. He died from diabetes. First, he went blind. Then the docs cut off one foot, then the other, then a leg, and then the other leg. Just whittling the poor guy down. I met him a few months before he died, when all his friends had abandoned him, and you know what, I never heard a word of complaint from him."

"I remember the things you wrote about him," I say. "It was hard stuff to read."

"Yeah," Cole says. "Hard to read . . . and even harder to write. But worse for him to live it."

I silently think to myself, '*Well, at least* **you** *didn't kill him, the guy who inspired you to be a writer, the guy you looked up to . . . at least you didn't cause his freaking death!*'

I've got to get us out of here.

It's getting colder. The dashboard of the Corvette, black and dead since we crashed, looks eerie. The faint images of the speedometer, the outline of the signal and instrument lights, and the tachometer on the control panel, make it look like the console of a frozen space ship. A ship littered with the bones of its dead crew, floating farther and farther into darkness, toward stars that will swallow it whole. That's how lonely it feels out here, even with Cole's company.

The forest has decided that it has nothing to fear from us. Insects, an owl, maybe a coyote or raccoon can be heard scrambling nearby in the darkness. In ways, the silence was more comforting. There is nothing that any wild animal could do to help us, but there may be ways it could harm us.

Cole rests, his eyes closed.

I start to doze off and, almost asleep, I accidentally move in a way I shouldn't. "Ahhhh," I cry out, biting my lip.

Cole opens his eyes. "Pretty bad, huh?"

I glance at the broken end of the bone sticking out of his pant leg and say, "It's nothing compared to how that must be feeling."

"I don't feel anything much," Cole says. "Just a little bit stiff and cold. Probably I'm in shock, but this doesn't feel any worse than any other times I've busted bones."

"Other times?"

"You work in slaughter houses, in warehouses and shipping departments, work with machines or on assembly lines or even sorting letters ten hours a day like the decade I spent with the post office—never mind all the bar fights I've been in—hell, you get hurt a lot. Are these the first broken bones you've had?"

"I'm not sure if I even broke anything."

"Sure you did," Cole says. "At least a couple ribs and that clavicle. It's going to get worse and worse the longer we're out here."

When he mentions how long we've been here, I ask, "How long do you think it's been?"

"Got to be an hour, at least. Hell, I've had time to tell you my whole life story including my philosophy about fame and fortune."

"Actually, you told me about fame before we crashed. You haven't talked about fortune at all yet."

"Oh, sorry," Cole says. "Here you go then—fortune is BS too."

"Come on . . ."

He laughs softly, flinching a little and putting his hand on his leg again, the white shard of bone circled by his thumb and palm. "I'm telling you, Ryan. You think that getting a big pile of dough will make you happy, will save you from something, but it doesn't. Some people believe that money is gonna make everything okay, that money will make life better. I've seen guys working sixty- and seventy-hour weeks, collecting all the overtime they could so that they can buy a little more crap. It's unbelievable what a man will do to himself—hell, what he'll do to *anybody* for money."

"That's easy for you to say. You're rich now."

"No, actually *now,* in terms of time and place, I'm trapped in a wrecked car with a kid who thinks fame and fortune will make life wonderful."

I stare down at my lap, biting my lip.

"Sorry, Ryan." Cole takes a slow, deep breath and continues, his voice giving away how much it hurts for him to speak. "Being rich is relative. When you're poor for most of your life, really poor, living in flophouses or hotels with bugs and rats or worse—out on the street—you think five bucks is a fortune, and it is. You have no idea, during times like that, what rich even means.

"Now, thanks to some good luck, I'm doing okay. My house is paid off, car is paid off, and I eat and drink and do pretty much whatever I want. But the truth is that money never meant that much to me anyway—maybe because I know what being poor is like and I know I can handle it. Also, I don't like to travel, don't like to go out to movies, dinners or parties. I hate all that crap that most people live for—can't stand to waste the time. I don't care about getting presents because the hassle and crap of giving somebody something back is too much to bear. There is so much crazy stuff that people do without thinking, because they think they *should* do it. Like having Granny over for Christmas, 'Come on Granny—come onnnnnnn,'" he says in a phony, sweet-sounding voice. But then, in his real voice, he quickly adds, "I'd rather *murder* myself."

Cole pauses for a moment and then continues. "The only thing having money does is give you one less thing to worry about, which is having enough money. I'll admit, that's a big thing for most people, but it's a far cry from a solution to most of their problems, and . . ."

A loud crackling sound interrupts him.

"Did you hear that?" I ask, my voice shaking.

He answers calm as ever, "How could I miss it?"

"What the . . ." I start to ask, my voice a panicked whisper. Adrenaline rushes through my body and brain. For these few seconds, I don't even feel my injuries.

Cole softly says, "Everybody loves nature . . ." He pauses and stares into the night. ". . . Until the fangs gather in the back of *their* necks."

10

We sit, me frozen and terrorized, Cole quiet, a strange smile on his face.

I try to control the fear in my voice. "What're we gonna do?"

Cole laughs softly. "Not a lot of options, Bucko. We're gonna wait and see what comes out of the dark."

"Jeez," I whisper.

"Relax, Ryan. It doesn't get any better than this."

I gulp and try to say okay, but the word won't come out.

I know that Cole is serious about *enjoying* this. I remember a poem he wrote about good and bad things, including good and bad ways to die, the best and the worst ways. He wrote that "Falling from the clouds . . . that's the best" and later in the poem, "In front of death squads . . . that's the best." Then, "Watching the bull gore the picador . . . that's the best."

In the darkness, a figure is moving around, the brush rattles, sticks and small twigs on the ground snap under its steps. What is it? I catch a glimpse of something moving like a shadow.

I'm petrified with fear. If I could run right now, and leave Cole here to be killed and eaten alive, I'd do it in a heartbeat . . . no, I couldn't do that . . . but I would, wouldn't I?

Yes.

No.

Maybe . . .

What do I mean, maybe? Am I really that cowardly? I'm too scared to think, too scared to even breathe. What if whatever is out there comes after me first? How can I be such a coward? All my life I've wanted to be special—famous, rich, something, anything more than the kid I see when I look in the mirror—but now, at crunch time, who am I? What am I? I don't need any mirror to see my fear, don't need any light to know how weak and selfish and hopeless I am. My father shot down enemy airplanes in war, killed people who were trying to kill him. How could I, weakling that I am, possibly be his son, of his blood and spirit?

Fear freezes me.

Cole says, "Hi there, Yogi."

Finally, as it steps towards us in the moonlight I can make it out. It's a bear, black as the night. Its eyes, visible in the moonlight, make it look demonic. Black bears, the only kind we have around here, rarely attack humans. They have cautious and careful demeanors. But this one stands in one spot, staring at us. It's not a huge bear, more like an adolescent, not quite full grown, but still big and formidable. Now it shifts back and forth, from one front leg to the other, as if readying to charge.

I find enough voice to finally speak. "Be careful, Cole."

Cole laughs.

I remember the end of his poem about the best and the worst things, "Plain old guts beating God-given talent . . . that's the best."

Before I can say anything more, the bear moves alongside the car on Cole's side, forcing its snout into the small hole where Cole's passenger window used to be. It must smell Cole's blood.

I want to scream, but before any sound comes out, Cole's left hand, fist tight and perfectly aimed, smashes into the bear's snout and broad face.

The animal grunts more than growls and, faster than you'd ever imagine it could move, it leaps back and hurries away, disappearing into the darkness.

Cole hollers after him, "Come on big boy, that all you got?" He laughs, but his laughter makes him jerk and grab his leg again, closing his eyes.

Embarrassed by my cowardice, not just some little

momentary flicker of fear, but my pure, total, chicken-butt, weak-ass, little-girl *terror*, I stay quiet.

Cole is quiet too. Talking helps me not think about my pain, but I'm too ashamed to say anything now . . .

This fix we're in is getting serious . . . not *getting* serious . . . it's been serious all along. What are we going to do? What am *I* going to do?

Still embarrassed at showing so much fear, I finally manage to mutter, "I'm sorry, I'm such a chicken, Cole. You were great."

He smiles. "Bravery is as relative as wealth, Ryan, and even more situational."

I don't get what he's saying. He's brave, I'm a coward. If nothing else, we just proved that. It seems pretty black and white to me, but I ask, "What do you mean?"

Cole says, "I'm not afraid of death especially, nor of being physically hurt. Growing up with my old man made me immune to that. But before my reading earlier tonight, did you know that I puked my guts out?"

I'm shocked. "You did? Why?"

Cole speaks softly, "Getting up in front of people, a spotlight shining into my face, strangers out there staring at me—I always puke before I have to go on stage."

I try to reassure him by telling him the truth. "You were great, Cole. Everybody loved you. Heck, they gave you a standing ovation."

"Sure, but it never holds for me. When I'm done and people are clapping and asking for autographs, I feel okay. But it never lasts. Before I even got to the car with you tonight, the terror of it all was back, thinking about having to go to the party, thinking about being around a bunch of strangers—that kind of crap is hell personified for me. I swear I'd rather have a root canal, rather be torn to shreds by a bear, than go into a room full of people I've never met."

I think about what Cole is saying, and I can't help but think how ironic it is. Here is this great writer, an incredible talent, who writes all the time but who hates the fame and attention it brings. And here I am, the exact opposite. A nobody-kid who has totally mixed feelings about actually writing, but who craves being the center of attention, who wants to be stared at by everybody and be the guy everyone wants to talk to, get close to. I'm terrified of *not* getting to be that someday.

Cole says, "So all I'm saying is that bravery isn't universal. Also, without being afraid of something, you never have a chance to be brave, to test yourself. And believe me, I'm terrified plenty, and I fail at finding bravery as much as anyone."

Cole's words bring me back from feeling as bad as I felt about myself a few moments ago—not all the way back, but a big part of it.

Still, what difference does any of that make if we don't get out of here? What difference does anything make? It's getting colder and scarier the longer we sit helpless. What are we going to do?

After a time of silence, Cole sighs, a strange sound, unlike any other he has made in all this time.

"You okay?" I ask.

"Better now," he answers.

I'm confused, until he adds, "I just took the astronaut option for taking a piss."

"The what?"

I see him smile through the darkness. "They don't have urinals in space little brother. We just go in our space suits."

I glance down and see the wet spot spreading across the front of his pants and I smile back. "Good move," I say. "This is no time to stand on proper etiquette."

Cole chuckles and says, "No time ever is."

11

We lie quietly for a long time, neither of us saying anything until Cole suddenly asks, "You hear that?"

"What?" I ask, confused. I think I was dozing, half-asleep, but I quickly wake up, wondering if the bear has returned. I ask again, "What is it?"

"Shush. Listen."

I concentrate . . .

We are both silent, and now I hear what Cole has heard. It's a vehicle on the road up above us, the road on which we were driving before we crashed!

"Car!" I yell, my ribs hurting as I raise my voice.

"Yep," Cole says, matter of fact, no excitement in his tone, as if the possibility we might be rescued means nothing to him.

"How can we signal it?" I ask.

"Look for his headlights, I guess. And when he's as close to us as he's gonna get, start yelling."

"Yeah."

I stare up towards the road and, in only a few seconds, light illuminates the trees and bushes, dim at first but brighter and brighter as the car comes closer. It's getting louder, and I feel its vibration as it moves towards us . . .

"Now, Cole!" I say, and both of us start hollering.

Cole yells, "HEYYYYYY!"

I scream, "HELPPPPPPPPP!"

The car seems to be going incredibly fast, its engine and the sound of its tires on the road and even the music from its radio roars over our puny cries. As quickly as it came, we catch a glimpse of taillight glow as the car speeds away. In seconds, it's gone.

"Do you think he heard us?" I ask.

"I doubt it."

Tears are in my eyes and my throat chokes. "How do you know?"

Calmly, Cole says, "Did you see his brake lights flash?"

"No."

"Don't you think if he'd heard something, he'd have slowed down, maybe tapped his brakes?"

I can't accept this. In all the time we've been here, this is the first and only car to come by. "Maybe he's going down the road to turn around and is coming back right now."

Cole looks at me and says, "Maybe," but I can tell he doesn't mean it.

Minutes pass and I hold my breath, listening and praying silently, *'Please God, let him come back . . . please make him save us.'*

More minutes go by and, finally, I know that Cole is right. The car is long gone. I feel depressed, hopeless, and scared. No one will ever see us here. No one will ever find us in time to rescue us. We're screwed, screwed, totally dead! Tears come to my eyes again.

Cole interrupts my self-pity. "You know, Ryan, I think you're gonna have to save us."

"How?"

"Where your window is broken out and the roof of the car is bent a little against the ground, there's that small space."

I glance at it. "Yeah, I've thought about that, but it's too small to squeeze through."

"Not if you dig under it, dig the dirt out from below where the top is pressing down towards the ground."

I look at what he's talking about, I get what he means, but it looks impossible. "I don't have anything to dig with."

Cole is quiet for a few seconds before he speaks again, his tone still calm and under control. "If I don't get some medical attention for this leg, I'm afraid I'll lose it. It was numb at first, but I'm starting to feel tingling up and down. It feels like it's dying." For the first time since we've been here, Cole sounds worried.

I take as deep a breath as my ribs and shoulder will allow, feel the white shock of pain stabbing me like it does with every breath, but finally I answer, "You think we can dig out and go find some help?"

Cole, calmly again, says, "I don't think there are any options. It won't be 'we' though. I can't be of any use to you digging, and even if you managed to pull me out, I can't walk. But if you can get out and go find help . . . hell, maybe your cell phone will even work once you're out of this little gully."

"I don't know, though . . ." I say as pain grabs and squeezes me when I reach with my right hand towards the small hole between where the window was and where the top is bent down. I pause a moment or two to let the pain subside. It hurts more than anything I've ever felt. But then I begin to gently scoop at the ground below the smashed roof. Even if I get a tunnel dug, I have no idea how I will be able to stand the pain of crawling out. Just getting out of my seat made me pass out. How will I stand this? But I guess I'll deal with that when I get to it . . . if I get to it.

12

Each small handful of dirt is paid for with excruciating pain. Not just the first few handfuls, but every one of them. I've been digging for I don't know how long—maybe ten minutes, maybe half an hour—but with each handful, pain smashes through my shoulder and the left side of my torso, almost paralyzing me.

I make a contest out of it, trying as hard as I can to not cry out or moan, trying not to complain or whine. Once every half a dozen or so scoops, this even works. Mostly though, I hear my voice, and it's as if the cries or grunts are coming from someone else—like I'm not really here.

Cole is quiet at first, but the more I moan, the more he talks to me. "If it's too hard, Ryan, just stop. We'll be alright."

He knows this isn't true and he knows that I know it too, so I keep digging. Before too long, I come across a rock about the size of my fist. It seems to take me forever to dig it out, but once I do, I see that it's shaped a little like a knife or a tiny shovel, much better for breaking the dirt loose than my already broken fingernails and sore, torn-up fingertips.

Sweat runs down my face even though the air is cold. At first, my hand ached from smashing into stones and roots hidden just below the surface. Now it feels numb, but the sharp stone is helping me make progress.

I feel like crying, like a coward and a baby. Why am I like I am? Why doesn't my dad love me more? How pansy-ass is that, oh poor me, Daddy doesn't love me . . . But I can't stop thinking it. I know my dad has a code, a sense of honor formed by a core of bravery. I've always disappointed him, or at least felt like I have.

Crap, piss, hell. Screw it, screw everything!

I hate these tears in my eyes. I keep my face turned away from Cole, so he won't see what a baby I am.

I'm digging around a large rock, and slowly, methodically removing tiny bits of dirt that hold it in place takes a long time.

Cole watches and comments, "You're doing great. That rock is your friend. Once you get it out, it'll leave a big hole on its own, that much less for you to have to dig."

After a while, Cole says, "Think about other things, good things."

I do as he suggests, thinking first about my bed back at home, my bedspread—orange and kind of old and ratty—but soft and warm. What I wouldn't give to be wrapped up in it right now, just dreaming all of this instead of living it.

Next, I think about Gabrielle Reid. She's gorgeous. When she laughs, it's like the sexiest, sweetest sound in the world. I think about her breasts and her hips. She doesn't even know me, but someday I hope she will. She's the kind of girl you'd die for. How can a guy be as whipped as I am over Gabrielle Reid when she doesn't even know that I exist? Next subject, please. This ain't exactly positive thinking, being too scared to ask out the girl of my dreams. Nice huh? Okay . . . *NEXT SUBJECT* . . .

Food . . . ahhhhhhh . . . Big Macs, that Thousand Island dressing they use and that half a bun in the middle. I realize I'm hungry, starving.

Good things though? Really, how long can a guy think about just *good things*? How many good things are there in the world? I don't want to sound negative, but come on. It seems to me that most of life isn't good things or bad things, but in-between things. Things like dinner, TV programs, boring classes, even at college where you'd think the people teaching would be really smart. Good things? What about hoof and mouth disease? What about the way most people drive? Good things? How can Cole Hardt, one of the most honest but cynical writers ever, suggest that I think about good things? I think there are limits to . . .

"Why poetry?" Cole interrupts my thoughts, maybe picking up my running-out-of-good-things vibe.

"Pardon me?"

"You said you're the poetry editor of your school magazine."

"Ye—" I stop mid-word from the pain in my shoulder.

Cole ignores my grimace, asking, "How'd you get interested in poetry?"

What can I say to Cole? Should I go into detail about my desire for fame? Wealth? Worldwide celebrity? No, he'd think I'm a jerk . . . heck, after listening to Cole talk about it earlier, *I think I'm a jerk* for that too. But I'm embarrassed to tell him the real reason I got interested in poetry, more than just embarrassed. I mean, it sounds like totally sucking up. I don't want to tell him, but it's the only answer that is totally true.

Finally, I admit it, "This probably sounds like I'm BS-ing you, but I got into poetry because of your poem, *Uncle Walt* about the Civil war and Walt Whitman and Lincoln."

I tell Cole the whole story, about Mr. James, our Intro to Lit Class, and how much I loved that poem.

"In fact," I confess, "I still remember most of it by heart . . . It's still one of my favorites."

There, I've said it. Cole can do whatever he wants with the news—tease me, laugh at me, or call me a sycophant. I don't really care.

He's quiet for a few moments before he finally says, "Thanks, Ryan." That's all he says, and I'm pretty sure that he's a little choked up.

"You're welcome," I answer.

Digging. You can hardly call what I'm doing digging. I have no tool except my one hand and my rock, and the amount of dirt I move with each effort is probably about a quarter of a cup, maybe a half-cup, but no more than that.

Frustrated, I say, "This is gonna take forever."

Cole says, "No, it'll take as long as it takes, and no longer. Forever is a long time."

"I was speaking metaphorically."

He smiles and says, "Try to avoid that when you can."

"I thought poets use metaphor all the time."

"Some do," Cole admits. "The *immortal* ones."

I laugh, but it hurts badly to laugh, so I also moan.

"Sorry," Cole says.

I think about how funny Cole is and it reminds me of his reading earlier tonight . . . that reading feels like it was a lifetime ago, but I still remember what he said about his humor.

In between a couple of his poems that the audience had laughed at and wildly applauded for, Cole explained, "I lived with a woman once who always told me I wasn't funny. But every time I was forced by financial desperation to go out and do a reading, people there would always laugh a lot. For a while, I couldn't figure it out—if I was so un-funny, how come people always laughed at what I said? But I finally got it. When I try to be funny, like most people who try to be funny, I'm not. When I tell the truth, the plain, simple truth as I see it, people are so surprised to hear it that they laugh involuntarily, a nervous laughter caused by the shock of hearing somebody say something that they already know to be true but that no one ever says out loud."

Still digging tiny handfuls of dirt, which I bring back into the wrecked Corvette and toss down into the spaces where the fastback glass used to be, I ask, "Cole, you said tonight that you think people laugh at hearing the truth?"

The truth to me right now is that I just want to keep him talking, partly for himself, but mostly for me. His words take me away from where I am, not so much to a different place (I wish), but to a different feeling inside myself, a place where I understand the world in different ways than ever before.

Cole repeats my question, "Do people laugh at hearing the truth? Well, first off, who knows what's true and what isn't? It's not so much my brilliant insights into truth with a capital T. God no. I am simply being honest. Most people, almost everybody, say what they think they should say, what's easiest to say. In the name of having a conversation, they ask you obvious crap, thinking they can predict what your answers will be. But when I'm honest with them, my answers don't square up with their expectations, and so they're surprised."

I think back to an example Cole gave during the reading, in front of the packed theater of fans hanging on his every word. I remember that he took a big slug off his wine bottle and then said, "Everybody likes a story. Say a guy walks into a bar all banged up and bleeding and he slumps down and orders a drink. Somebody says, kindly, 'Hey, Buddy, tough day?' And the beat-up guy says, 'It's a long story . . .' Point being, everybody in the bar now REALLY wants to hear it, because stories, especially true stories, are the things that give meaning to life . . .

"When you answer honestly," he told the audience, "people don't know what to say back, so they laugh."

As I was listening to Cole earlier, I had wondered, and now ask him, "How can you live in the world if you don't try to be nice to people at least some of the time?"

"Nice?" Cole says, like it's a word he doesn't understand.

I don't back down. "Yeah, *nice*. Like you're being to me right now?"

"I'm not being nice to you, Ryan. I'm talking to you because we're here together. If we were in some other environment, maybe I'd still be talking to you, but if we were at a party, where I always feel self-conscious and crappy, I'd be drinking, drinking a lot. And if there was some dame there who had that certain look in her eye, that look that says, 'I'm interested in you . . . come here and you might find something that will make you happy or you might end up being butchered like the pig you are, then . . .' Sorry, Ryan, but I guarantee that you'd be staring at my back as I headed straight into the flame."

I smile, dropping another tiny handful of dirt, "Straight into the flame, huh? Isn't that a metaphor too?"

Cole chuckles and grimaces. "I wish."

13

It's cold. Not a little chilly, not pleasantly brisk—it's friggin' freezing. Every time Cole says something, or I say something back, our breath turns to mist. But I've made a lot of progress on the little tunnel, and now it might be big enough to wiggle through.

Cole stares at it and says, "You ready to give it a try?"

I hesitate, then say, "Yeah, I think so."

"It's gonna hurt."

"Yeah."

We're both silent until Cole says, "When I was a kid, a few years younger than the age you are now, I had a little bout of cancer. Leukemia to be exact. For about ten months I had to go through all the treatment. I got on chemo and radiation, and my hair fell out, eyebrows and all. I had to go in and see the cancer docs every week, riding the city bus to my appointments because both my parents worked. Most times, being there alone, all bald and self-conscious,

I'd just sit and stare down into my lap, trying to ignore the stares, the blatant gaping of strangers. I'd try not to hear their whispers about what a freak I was.

"Finally, I beat the cancer, although I had to be checked for it all through junior high and high school. I must have had a million needle pricks and thrown-up a hell of a lot of times, but it was the scars on the inside of me that never left. But after a while, and still to this day, I became proud of those scars. They remind me of everything that the pain gave to me and made of me. Not the pain of the chemo and radiation and all that crap, but the pain of so-called *normal* people being as thoughtless and cruel as those strangers were to a sixteen-year-old kid suffering something amazingly difficult, something that they could never even imagine, much less understand unless they'd been through it themselves."

I'm not sure why Cole is telling me this. In talking about pain, does he want me to know that he understands what pain is too? Is he saying that what I'm going through right now could be a lot worse? Is he giving me a pep talk? No matter what he says, it's going to hurt like hell to try to drag my body through this tiny hole in the ground and then go for help. And I don't know if I can do it.

Again, like he's done so many times since I've met him, Cole seems to read my mind. But now when he speaks, his voice is more firm—not angry really, but matter-of-fact.

"I know you're afraid of the pain, Ryan. I get that. But in every guy's life there comes a moment where he has to stop hiding behind Mommy's apron and deal with things. This could be that moment for you, whether you want it or not. Earlier, when that bear came, and we talked about bravery, that's a different thing than what I'm talking about now. Bravery that flows from instinct or just reflex-reaction is easy. Character is different than that. There are guys you want at your back in life and guys you wouldn't trust to pick up your laundry. It's not that the one guy is good and the other bad. It's never that simple. No one sets out to be weak. No one gets up in the morning, looks in the mirror, and says, 'I wonder how many lies of conscience and pain-avoiding short-cuts I can take today?'

"The truth is, nobody knows if they're going to be a stand-up guy until the chance to test yourself arises. How can a guy know what he's made of until he's tested? You seem like a good kid, Ryan, but 'good kid' isn't going to cut it now. 'Good kid' time is done. It's time to see whether or not you can be something more than that."

As Cole speaks, his tone—his stern, clear voice—reminds me of my dad's voice. When my dad talks to me like this, I've always thought that he's just being my parent, doing his job at *raising me right* with boring lectures, and I've always hated that. As Cole speaks it's obvious that he doesn't care about my feelings. He isn't concerned about what I think or what I might say back or even what I might do. He's just saying that some guys step up when the time comes, and some don't. How come I can hear Cole say the same thing my dad has said to me in a thousand different ways but couldn't really hear?

My right hand, covered in scratches and cuts and filthy and freezing cold from digging, hurts a lot. But that pain is nothing compared to my ribs and my left shoulder.

"There's one other thing, Ryan, something I've got to say . . ." Cole's tone has changed, back to how he sounded before. He speaks in a softer voice, pausing as I look over. After maybe half a minute, as though he is searching for the words, he finally says, "Ryan, you're young and strong and you'll be okay if you make yourself fight through your pain. Without your help, though, I don't know how long I can last. I hate to sound melodramatic, but I've lost a fair bit of blood and I don't know how much more of this cold I can take."

When Cole mentions being cold, I realize just how much colder it is. It's probably not quite freezing, but it's close to it. And trapped in this wrecked car, with no protection from the night air and lying here immobile so close to the cold ground, we could soon be in trouble with hypothermia—if we're not already.

But I can tell that Cole isn't scared. He sounds just like he sounded earlier when talking about other things, asking me about my dad, telling me about fame and wealth, saying he wished he didn't have to go to the party. No, it's not fear behind Cole's words. His tone matches what he's saying.

"I don't want to die out here," he says. "But that isn't my biggest interest. My focus is on getting to watch you step up. You can do this."

I breathe as deeply as I can. "I'll go get us help, Cole. I'll go in just a minute—I will."

Cole just nods.

I don't say anything more as I stare at the small hole I've dug running underneath where the driver's side window used to be.

I'll have to turn my body at an almost impossible angle, belly to the ground so I can use my good arm to drag myself through. There's no other way.

I look back at Cole and say, "Okay, sit tight. I'll be back with the cavalry as soon as I can."

Cole smiles and says, "I've always preferred the Injuns for this kind of job, but you grab the first guy you see and get us the hell out of here."

"You got it," I say, trying to sound brave. I look at the hole again and try to not think what I am thinking . . .

Man, this is going to be bad!

I had passed out from the pain when I undid my seatbelt. Once that belt let me go, I fell as much as slid down, unable to control how fast I moved. But as I move into the little tunnel to pull myself forward until free, I will have the ability to move in small increments.

I study the angles, think about the position of my legs and the best way to make my body move. I manage to lift my left arm a little, but the pain is too much. By holding my left elbow snugly against my side, I can put a light pressure on my ribs, holding them in place. By applying that pressure, both my shoulder and the left side of my torso feel a tiny bit better.

My concentration is so good that when Cole asks, "Anything I can do to help?" I jerk and look at him. I'd forgotten he was here.

"No," I answer. "I'm good."

I concentrate again on my plan for moving and realize, "Cole I'm gonna have to move my legs so they're in your space when I'm crawling out."

"Sure," he says.

"I don't want to hit your leg and hurt you."

I can hear the smile in Cole's voice. "Don't worry about that. I'll grab hold of your legs and make sure they don't bang into my wound. Also, that way I'll be able to push you forward if you need it."

"Don't push me unless I ask," I say quickly. "I'll control the speed."

"Okay," Cole says.

I take one more breath, and now a couple more. Not deep breaths—that would kill me right now—but slow, steady breaths. It's now or never.

I say to Cole, "Let's do this."

"Yep," he says.

Pain is not my master, pain is not my master, pain is just pain . . . it means nothing . . . Jesus Christ on his cross . . . pain is the sliver embedded deeply in your finger and the needle digging it out from bright red infection. Pain has no consciousness, nor conscience. It isn't thoughtful, it isn't cruel—it's just here, a part of life. Right now, my pain is tall and strong and relentless, but it isn't alive. It's just in my mind. Pain isn't real, it's just a fantasy, a bad dream . . . You can tell yourself whatever you want as you try to turn your mind away from pain, away from agony, but it's still here, of course.

Suddenly, I think about the title of one of Cole's great books: *What Matters Most Is How You Walk Through the Flames.* It's my favorite of all of Cole's titles, words I've never quite understood: what matters most is how you walk through the flames . . . I said the line to my dad once and he nodded and smiled.

Pain, pain, pain . . . my whole world is on fire in pain . . . a world about only one thing, trying to walk through the flames of pain . . . I can't escape pain, but I can challenge it, beat it back . . . think about other things . . .

What do I love? What do I fear? What kind of boy have I been? What kind of man will I be?

There is my father's face . . . my mother's hands . . . why am I being tortured, killed . . . no, not killed, I'm not dying from this, I'm just hurting . . . a lot . . . *A LOT!*

My head is through the hole, dirt rubbing into my face, on my nose and lips—dirt, which I spit away. I am coming out of the womb of the earth, a newborn baby, arriving from pain . . . My neck and finally my shoulders move into the birth canal, not sliding at all. My body wants to stick, but I pull myself forward, dragging with both hands at first until my left side screams pain at me, screams it too loud and clear to be ignored. I place my left arm back where it must go, pressing lightly against my left side and holding my body together. With just my right arm, digging my fingers into the earth as if hanging from a cliff, I pull myself, tiny movements, a centimeter, a few millimeters, almost too small a distance to detect, but moving, dragging, crawling, slow, so slow. Through this pain, I am being born out into the world . . .

Tears stream down my face. But I ignore them. They are nothing. I am nothing . . . just my pain, just my slow

slow slow slow movement forward. Each inch is a battle won. Each stab of pure white pain is a message reminding me of who I am . . . I am the guy crawling through flames, in spite of my fear, the fear of giving up, the fear of failing . . . what matters most is how you walk through the flames . . . I can't give up . . . I won't . . .

Finally, my hips squeeze out, and my ribs and shoulder on my left side scream at me to stop. My head, arms, hips, legs, knees, ankles, and feet feel numb and cold and disconnected from me. Me, I am just my pain and the places where I ache. No, I am more than that!

"How's it going kid?" Cole calls to me.

"Okay," I mutter, even though it hurts to say this much.

"Looks like you're getting there," Cole encourages.

I don't want to hurt anymore . . . I don't want to be anything . . . Just to stop hurting.

My face, still pressing down onto the ground, feels cold. Rocks, twigs, small stones, and dried leaves scrape against me. I breathe slowly, trying to get enough oxygen to move again . . . but I'm so tired . . . too tired . . . weak, too weak . . . I close my eyes . . .

I am floating . . .

. . . *Cole and I are at the party, and he is drinking heavily, and I am watching him . . . for some reason, I can remember every poem he ever wrote . . . how can this be? I know how, they are MY poems. Cole stole them all from me! Wait, that*

makes no sense, but it feels true. I am the poet. I am the best.
Everyone loves me, and now gorgeous women begin to stare at
me, but I realize that I'm not wearing any pants . . . I have
no underwear on either . . . why did I go commando tonight?
Cole looks at me and says, "Relax, Ryan. Every poet is naked
when he writes honestly. Don't worry . . . also . . ."

"Ryan," I hear Cole calling.

I wake up and realize that I've been unconscious,
dreaming. I'm not naked from the waist down after all,
thank God. I am back to reality and I mutter to Cole, "I'm
okay."

"Good," Cole says, his voice sounding weak.

"Are you alright?"

"My leg is hurting more." Again, he speaks in the
calmest tone, no hint of self-pity, but he's weak, using
almost no breath at all.

"I'm getting there, Cole," I call back. "I'll go find help.
Hang tight."

Cole mumbles something which I can't make out.

"I'm almost out, Cole."

"Good," I hear from behind me, weaker even than his
previous few words.

From my knees, panting like a wounded animal, I try to stand, rising only an inch or two. The worst pain so far rips through me, worse even than when I undid my seatbelt and fell—worse than any pain ever. I collapse back onto my hands and knees. I should say *hand* not *hands* because although I try to put my left hand down, it hurts too much. It can't take any weight at all. Only my right hand can stand the pressure. I balance on my knees and right hand, like a tripod, holding onto the ground to keep the swirl of pain from pushing me over.

Strange, this pain is the worst I've felt, yet I don't pass out. I grab the earth and force my breathing low and calm, steady and easy, and now it's almost as if the pain is under some of my control.

How am I going to stand? I have to stand up to find us help, don't I? Yes, of course I do. There are no houses in the forest for miles, no help unless a car comes by again. But how can I go if I'm crawling and don't even know where I'm crawling to? If I could see a house, a light, anything to give me some direction, I could crawl that far. But I know this road too well. There's nothing for miles, and I can't crawl forever. I have to try to stand again, have to force myself to my feet.

It's going to hurt too much . . . Doesn't matter. I have to do it. *What matters most . . .* God, just let me do this . . . God, help me please . . .

I take several breaths and am almost ready to try to force myself to my feet again when I think I hear Cole behind me "*. . . carrying burdens of unimaginable weight . . .*"

"What?" I call back.

Silence.

Am I hallucinating?

"What?" I yell again.

He doesn't reply, but I think I can hear him breathing harder. I use his silence as my excuse not to try to stand again. Tears fill my eyes when I try to speak. They choke back my voice. I'm terrified to cough, scared to even clear my throat.

Finally, I croak out, "I'm afraid to stand up."

There's no response.

"Cole," I call.

Silence.

I don't want to write poems.

I don't want to write anything.

I don't want to get famous, so that I can make love to beautiful girls.

I don't care about money.

I don't care about being on TV.

I don't care about seeing my name in print.

I don't care about anything.

I don't care about my long hair.

I wish my dad were here to help me.

I don't care about living anymore . . . no, that's not true. I care about that. It's all I care about right now . . . living . . . and saving Cole.

Dad . . . please . . . Dad . . .

What I care about now is as real as it gets—being the person my father wants me to be, the guy I need to be.

And now, as I kneel here, hurting worse than I have ever hurt before, calling in my mind for my Dad's strength and help, a memory washes over me, a memory of Dad and me . . .

It was a summer day. I was twelve. Mom and Dad and I were in the woods at our lake place, on our way to a favorite picnic spot—a small, cool waterfall that hardly anybody knows about.

We were almost to our destination, the sound of the waterfall kind of faint but building as we got closer. That's when we saw, a dozen feet off the path and lying on the ground, a small gray and brown coyote whose leg was caught in a steel trap. There was a lot of blood soaking into the ground, some of it already dry. The animal had a horrified look in its eyes, scared and hurt, in pain and dying. Half his leg had been chewed through in his effort to escape the trap.

My father cursed softly, and then said to Mom, "Honey, you go on ahead."

Mom looked at Dad, and without saying a word, she walked on.

"Should I go too?" I asked my dad.

"No," he said. "You stay and help me, okay?"

I gulped but said, "Sure," standing silently next to him.

Once Mom was out of sight, Dad removed his jacket and slowly approached the wounded animal. I saw Dad's jaw set.

"Are we going to save him?"

Dad looked at me and said, "It's too late. He's pretty much bled out. We're going to end it."

For a second, I was confused. "End it?"

Dad didn't answer. Instead, he slowly draped his jacket over the coyote's head, speaking gently to him. "It's okay, boy. Relax. Easy does it."

Dad softly stroked the coyote's back and sides. At first, the animal jerked around some, but soon it lay still and quiet.

I asked, "Are you going to kill it?"

"That's all we can do, son."

"Can't we just let it go?"

He pointed to the ground around the coyote. "See all that blood? This animal is not going to live much longer, and it's wrong to let it suffer. The most humane thing to do is end it."

I nodded like I agreed, but I felt sorry for the coyote and angry with my dad, even though I knew that what he said was right.

Dad said, "You can look away, son, if you want to. There's no shame in that. This is an ugly thing, a bad deal."

I nodded but chose to watch what Dad did next. He lifted the coyote's head, still covered by the jacket, and gripped the animal's muzzle. Then, in one violent motion, he put his knee on the coyote's shoulder and gave the head a hard twist. I heard a sickening crack and quickly looked away. When I looked back, the coyote lay still—like a stone, like a piece of old wood, like something that had never been alive at all. I've seen ten-thousand fake TV deaths, like everybody, but they never looked like this.

After a moment, Dad said, "If you have the stomach for it, I'll show you how to get this trap off."

"Okay," I answered in a daze. It was all too awful. I glanced at the coyote for a moment as Dad removed his jacket and I wished I hadn't. Its eyes were clouded already, a layer of milky film covering them. The nostrils had small spots of blood. I noticed that Dad's jacket had some blood on it too, a few drops on one of the sleeves.

Dad pried the trap open and lifted it up and gave it a soft shake. The coyote fell out and made a small thump as it hit the ground. Dad picked up the coyote by its rear legs and walked away. I followed. We went some distance from where the trap had been, and Dad laid the body down gently in thick, deep underbrush. We walked back, and Dad picked up the trap and wrapped it in his jacket and carried it with us as we walked the rest of the way to meet up with Mom.

At the edge of the waterfall, standing on the rocky bank, Dad took the trap out of his jacket and tossed it downstream into the middle of the river where the white water churned and the mist rose up.

I stood silently next to Dad. I kept staring at the spot where the trap had landed and sunk into the dark river.

Dad said, "Sometimes a guy has to do an ugly, hard thing. The only saving grace is doing it right the first time, doing it so that it's over and done. You tell yourself that you can do it—not that you want to, but it's what you have to do, so you do it and you do it properly. When it's over, you know that you did your best. Sometimes that's all you're going to get out of it, so it's got to be enough."

My dad's not the kind of guy who gives speeches—I

mean, never—and I didn't really understand in that moment by the waterfall what he meant. But now I get it . . .

"Sometimes a guy has to do an ugly, hard thing" . . . "You tell yourself you can do it" . . . "When it's over, you know that you did your best . . ."

What Dad said—and what Cole knows too—I am learning right now. Fame and fortune are nothing except words, and while words mean a lot, there are things that words don't and can't say—things like doing what you have to do when the time comes to prove yourself. A good writer knows when words are enough, and a good man knows when life demands more than just words.

Staring back at the wrecked Corvette, I take two short breaths and mutter a silent, quick prayer, "Let me do this, God."

I push myself up with my right hand onto quivering legs—a slow, awful motion, rising in the smallest increments. Pain stabs me harder. My left elbow is still tucked gently against my ribs to hold my body together, left hand on my belly. I rise, leaning forward, hunched over but finally standing on my own two feet. My numb legs are throbbing back to life but holding me upright.

I try to call to Cole, try to tell him I'm standing, but it hurts too much to speak. Just hold on now, just stand still and breathe slowly, get my bearings, get my balance. I glance around on the ground for a stick to use like a cane or crutch, but there's nothing anywhere nearby.

Finally, to Cole, I holler, "I'm up . . . on my feet . . . I'll go . . . find help." My voice is weak. It's hard to talk without being able to breathe.

Cole doesn't answer. He hasn't answered for how long now?

"Yeah," I mutter, speaking so softly that I can barely hear myself. "I'll go get help, Cole."

And again, silence.

I'm not what you'd call an intimidating figure, bent over
like a thousand-year-old man. I stare up at the steep bank I
am going to have to climb. I focus on what I've just done,
on making it out of the car and standing.

I want to call back to Cole again, but I don't have the
energy. I'm going to have to use all my strength to get out
of here.

There is no path up the embankment to the road. It's
overgrown in waist-high bushes. I start to wade into them
and feel the sting of thorns through my pant legs and on
my hands as I nudge the branches out of my way.

"Wild roses," I mumble.

I realize that even though we have wild roses right
behind our fence back home, I've never stopped and
smelled them before. 'Stop and smell the roses, huh?' I sniff
the air but can't smell any rose scent, and my legs are too

shaky, my body too sore, to bend over further and get a closer sniff.

Unable to grab the thorny branches of the bushes, I have to rely on my footholds and balance to keep moving up the hill. Each time I lift and push with my legs, pain shoots through me. Each strike of the pain seems just like the one before it—nothing I can't handle, nothing I haven't already survived. But could this pain be cumulative? Could it build and build until finally one of the shocks will drop me to my knees? Might it be easier to crawl up this hill? But the thorns on these bushes are sharp and would that pain be too much to bear?

As I'm pondering this, I realize that I've reached the top of the steep drop-off and that I am already on the side of the road. I steady myself again, imagining how much it would hurt to lose my balance and fall all the way back down. I glance behind me. I can't see the car. Is this all a nightmare? What's going on? Where's Cole?

"Cole," I yell, as loud as I can.

But again, damned silence. I stare hard into the darkness and I can finally make out the top of one of the tires and part of the black undercarriage of the vehicle. No wonder that car didn't see us before—we're almost invisible.

I call back to Cole again, "I'm on the road, Cole. I'll find help."

He doesn't answer.

"Cole," I yell again.

Still no answer. Is he calling back, but I just can't hear? Did he pass out again?

"Cole . . . Cole!" I yell, as loud as I can.

Nothing.

Goosebumps cover my arms, and the hair on the back of my neck stands up. My injuries, when I stand here perfectly still, don't hurt as much, but I don't have the strength to go back down there to check on him. I have to move along the road until I find help.

I keep repeating silently, over and over again, 'Please, Cole, be all right . . . please, be okay . . .'

I'm not sure which way to go. Are we past the top of the hill or were we still on the upward climb when we went off the road? In the dark, it's hard to tell for sure which way is up and down, but staring hard into the darkness, I'm almost certain that we were headed down, moving towards the Idaho State line.

I try my cell, and there's still no signal. There are trees everywhere, and I know from hundreds of trips along this road to our lake place in Bayview, Idaho, that cell reception is always weak in these mountains. After a few minutes of trying, my cell phone screen goes black. I stupidly left the phone on the whole time we've been out here. It's been searching for a signal, and now the battery's dead.

I have to move towards help, a cabin or a small house somewhere tucked into the woods. I have to move towards the town of Blanchard far up ahead. I have to go.

Walking is hard. Each step hurts. But after that first step, I manage a couple steps, then I'm able to do a couple more, then half a dozen, and finally a full dozen. I pause, breathe rapidly but not too deeply, and take a dozen more steps, thinking silently, over and over, *I'll get us help, Cole . . . I'll find help and come back for you.*

I take note, pay attention to the first mile marker post I come to, number 82. It's only fifty yards or so down from the crash site. I'll be able to find my way back here to Cole. I've got it. I know where I am.

I call back to Cole again. Still, nothing but silence . . .

I'll make it. I have to make it.

I move on . . .

18

After walking for a while, everything starts to blur together. It feels like I've been walking for two or three hours—I don't know.

Finally, I see headlights approach and then slow down. It's a pickup truck, and someone is talking to me. This all feels like a dream, but why would I dream of two drunk guys in a beat-up truck?

I ask the driver if he has a cell phone and he laughs, saying, "We're out here spotlighting deer, not a great need for cellular communications. Besides, you can never get a signal on this back side of the mountain."

Finally, I pull open the passenger door and haul myself in. The young guy scoots over to make room and offers me a beer.

"No, thanks," I say, and begin to describe the crash, my injuries, and that Cole is still in the car. This seems to sober the guys up right away.

The driver asks, "Should we go back for your buddy?"

"We're going to need serious help," I explain. "If you can just get me to a phone, please."

"You bet," the passenger answers. Then he turns to the driver and says, "Pedal to the metal, Floyd."

And Floyd floors it.

The town of Blanchard is buttoned-down for the night. A digital clock on the Banner Bank sign shows 12:49. The only place open is a tavern with a large glowing sign attached to the front of the cinder block building. The sign reads, *Charlie My Boy,* and there's a cartoon of a round-faced drunk with a bulbous red nose wearing a vest and a top hat. The guy looks a little like a cartoon caricature of Cole.

The tavern isn't crowded, but all eyes turn to watch me as I walk in, leaning over, my left arm tucked against my side.

The bartender starts to ask, "You got any ID? We . . ." He pauses mid-sentence, looking at me more closely. "You got a bunch of twigs and crap in your hair, son—"

"Call 911," I interrupt.

My head starts to spin . . . I mumble Cole's name . . .

I hear myself say, "A wrecked Corvette . . . mile marker 82 . . . send help . . . call my dad."

And then I'm floating and . . . sinking onto the floor . . . and everything goes black . . .

19

I wake up several times in the ambulance on the way to Kootenai County Medical Center in Coeur d'Alene, Idaho. And I'm awake and feeling much less pain because of the medicine they're giving me when Cole finally arrives. He is hurriedly wheeled into a nearby spot in the Emergency Room, where the nurses pull blue curtains around him, followed by a flurry of people racing in and out.

It turns out that part of his left femur has sheared off, missing his femoral artery by only a quarter of an inch and creating his fracture. Rather miraculously, most of the femur is undamaged, and so the break isn't nearly as bad as it could have been.

I've broken ribs 2-3-4-5 and 7-8 on my left side, plus I fractured my left clavicle, just like Cole had thought. They run a CAT scan to make sure that my spleen isn't ruptured and my lungs aren't punctured, and I've been lucky there too—no further damage to either other than a deep bruise on the lung.

Mom and Dad come to sit at my bedside in the hospital. When I tell Dad how sorry I am about his car, he just smiles and says, "That's why we have insurance." He never would say another word about it to me.

I'm released from the hospital after one night. They've given me some terrific painkillers, and within a couple days I'm able to visit Cole while he is recovering. We talk a lot, but only one time about writing.

Cole asks me to bring him some of my stuff to read. I'm nervous as all hell, and it turns out I should be because he reads half a dozen of my poems, then lays the folder aside and is quiet for a few moments before he finally speaks.

"This isn't very good, Ryan," he says directly and without emotion.

I feel myself blush and start to say, "I . . . um . . ."

Cole cuts me off. "You got the words here, kid. Your smarts come through, but good writing is only partly about being smart, and not even the most important part. I don't feel you in here. I don't feel anybody in here. You're just jerkin' the words off, being clever and smart—and the thing is, you're a kid, so you can bet your ass there're a lot cleverer and smarter writers out there than you are now."

I nod and I'm afraid to make eye contact with him,

until he says, "Don't worry about it. Like I said, you're still just a kid. You got time, and with any luck at all, life will kick the shit out of you enough to where you'll find that way to make us feel you, to make us feel, period."

He pauses a moment and smiles. "Consider those ribs of yours, and me laid up here as Life Lesson Number 1 in what will be an ongoing horror show."

But most of my visits and most of our talks are not about writing, not about fame or fortune—more just about regular life and about the accident. Mostly, Cole needs to sleep and rest, so the visits are always pretty short.

Early in the evening of Cole's fourth day in the hospital, my dad, who has driven me there each day but has stayed out in the waiting area, finally joins Cole and me. Dad and I walk into Cole's room just as he's finished eating dinner, the little table with his hospital tray and empty plates pushed to the side of his bed.

Cole looks the best he's looked since he's been here. His face is a little bit red but way better than the pale, blue-around-the-gills look he had the first days. His hair is combed, and when he sees me his eyes kind of light up.

"There he is," Cole says. "The kid who almost killed Hardt."

He's called me this a few times now. At first, I kind of shuddered when I heard it, but now I smile.

"Cole," I say, "This is my dad, Alan."

Cole puts out his hand for my dad to shake, which he does. I notice that their grips look firm, kind of macho actually.

Dad says, "Nice to meet you Mr. Hardt."

"Cole, please."

"Cole," my dad says with a subtle smile.

"Sorry about your car, man."

"Not to worry. It's only a car."

"Bullshit," Cole says. "It was a Corvette, a fiberglass body extension for guys with fears of adequacy . . ."

Dad's smile disappears, and there's this tense moment until Cole adds, "Those cars make your arms feel bigger, right?"

They both laugh.

Coles says, "It was a beautiful machine, Alan, and I've never met a Corvette owner who didn't love his car almost as much as he loves his kids."

Dad, still smiling says, "Yeah, but only almost."

"Yeah," Cole says. Then he nods at the chairs at the end of his bed and asks us to sit.

We pull up the chairs and get as comfortable as we can, which isn't easy for me with my ribs and shoulder. Even with my pain medicine, I can't clear my throat, cough, or laugh without it feeling like somebody's stabbing me in the chest with an icepick.

Our conversation is nothing special. Cole and Dad swap a few stories. Cole talks about being a writer as if it was the same as being a plumber or a salesman. "Just a way to make the nut each month," he says. Cole asks Dad about his work as an accountant and seems to take a genuine interest, asking about taxes, financial regulations, job growth, and the national debt, and listening while my dad talks accountant talk—blahblahblah.

After half an hour or so, I notice Cole pressing the little button which lets him medicate himself. He's on an IV that drips pain killers through a tube into his arm.

He smiles at me and says, "Gonna be 'last call' pretty quick."

I nod. From my earlier visits I know that once he presses that little plunger and his meds kick in, his eyes get droopy pretty quickly.

My dad says, "We should let you get some rest anyway, Cole."

Cole smiles but quickly says, "One more thing though, Alan."

Dad stops and looks down at Cole, waiting.

Cole says, "When I was a kid, my old man was an abusive piece of shit. He used to come out after I'd mow the yard and measure the blades of grass, actually measure them with a twelve-inch ruler. And if he found a single blade longer than any of the other ones, which the son of a bitch ALWAYS found, of course, then he'd take me back into the house and beat me with a razor strap."

I flash back to flipping my dad off behind my back that time he made me re-mow the yard, and I feel like that was a thousand years ago, back when I was a spoiled brat and stupid child.

I had read about Cole's father many times in his writings and hearing him tell it to my dad rips into me, stabs at my heart, and brings tears to my eyes.

But Cole's voice is steady, as though he is telling us something that he refuses to let hurt him any longer. "I hated my old man, and his brutality made me who I became—a lot of bad things, yet some good ones too. I learned from him that strength doesn't come from love alone. Sometimes, strength comes from inside a person when that person has to face the worst."

Cole pauses a moment and then says, "Ryan saved our lives out there, Alan. No two ways about it. What he did was hard and heroic and a thousand times braver than anything I ever did in my life."

I'm almost afraid to look at my dad, but when I do, I see that he has tears in his eyes too.

In that same detached, monotone voice, Cole says, "Any man who has raised a kid who could do what Ryan did out there in the woods—keeping it together, digging his way out of that wreck despite the pain, never giving up—any man who raises a kid like that has done something special."

My dad stares down for a moment or two, and I can tell that he's trying to compose himself, get his emotions under control. Finally, Dad says, "Thanks, Cole. I appreciate that."

There's a pause, not long enough to get uncomfortable, but long enough for Cole's eyelids to almost close before he jerks awake.

"One more thing, Alan," Cole says.

"Sure," Dad answers.

"Any chance you can rustle me up a bottle of Scotch or a six-pack of beer somewhere?"

Dad looks at Cole who manages to hold his deadpan expression for only a few seconds before breaking into a laugh. When Dad realizes that Cole's just teasing him, he smiles and says, "We'll have to see what we can do about that."

The next morning Cole is released from the hospital, and that same afternoon he flies back home to Southern California. He doesn't say goodbye.

20

Two years later, Cole Hardt died.

Leukemia.

It happened so fast. The death notice in *Time* Magazine called him "the poet laureate of skid row" and said that he had been diagnosed only a few months before. I had never spoken to him or heard from him again after he went back to Los Angeles.

I stuck with writing until a miracle happened—I learned to love it. This began almost right after I got home from the accident. Words no longer felt like enemies. Instead of boredom, it became a true interest, which soon grew into a passion. Cole was right about writing—that the doing of it is truly the best part.

A few weeks after Cole died, I went to the mailbox one afternoon at the student-housing apartment where I live now with my girlfriend Gabrielle Reid, at Eastern Washington University. Yeah, *that* Gabrielle Reid. At first, she seemed to like me mostly because of all the attention I got after the accident, but somewhere along the way she turned into a *real* girlfriend, someone who, despite being drop-dead gorgeous, actually has a brain and a heart. Who'd have thunk it? I'm a Creative Writing major and Gabrielle wants to be a Special Ed teacher.

I thumbed through the mail that day. There were all the usual offers for credit cards, a flier from the local Safeway grocery store, and a few other pieces of garbage. I was ready to throw it all away when I noticed in the return address spot on an envelope half-hidden by the others the single hand-written word, *Hardt*.

I opened it immediately:

Hey Ryan,

I know it's been a while since we've seen each other. If you're getting this, that means my ass is boxed up and planted by now. Hopefully, you've already heard the news.

No, this isn't coming from the great beyond. It's something I had in my desk for a while but never got around to sending. I left directions that it should be mailed to you. So if you have it, consider this as one tiny bit of evidence that all of mankind isn't always completely hopeless (just most people, most of the time, and crowds always).

I remembered how much you liked my poem about Uncle Walt and Abraham Lincoln. I thought you might like this enclosed poem too. It seems especially suitable to our present situation. Don't bother to memorize it, buddy—that's why we write them down, remember?

Your pal,
Cole

P.S. In case I never mentioned it, thanks for saving my life.

On another sheet of paper, in the same handwriting as the note:

Walt Whitman and the Sparrows

At the hour of his death
Walt Whitman knows that it's
the sparrows that provide the litmus test—
Not the birds themselves
But his ability to render them—

119

"Did you notice sparrows?" Will be the question
asked by the universe,
And Walt will answer:
"I saw their brown wings
The intricate web of patterns
Leading one feather to the next—
The yellowish beak and their breasts...
(Were they tan or gray or beige?
Something like that,
Sorry I'm not quite sure)
Their tiny clawed feet
gripping a wire, a branch,
a top fence rail—
And in May I saw their mouths dripping
With green twigs, leaves,
Brown grass for building nests—"
    "What else?" The universe will insist.
"Well, their songs, of course,
Their chirp, chirp, chirp—
and their skittish nervous motion
like pine cones quivering on high tree limbs
when the wind picks up.
Yes, the sparrows did not escape me—
I heard their breath, and
Felt their softness

And let myself turn into their flight—
I remember them well—
The sparrows, yes."

   "Okay, Walt,"
The universe will answer,
"Close enough."

AFTERWORD

Last week, I got my first poem published, and believe it or not, the magazine is going to actually *pay* me for it. Okay, I admit it's only a few bucks, but I'm determined that it won't be the last poem of mine ever to find its way into print.

I hope readers can feel this poem.

I hope that somewhere, somehow, Cole can feel it too.

Riding with Cole

I am riding
In an imaginary car
With the ghost
Of Cole Hardt.
We're silent
For the moment,
Him because he has

Nothing to say,
Me because I'm in awe.

I've been instructed,
Guided,
Inspired
By his work forever,
And here we are,
Finally,
Together
Once again.
Never mind that he died
A few years ago.

Studying the deep creases
Of pain
And wounds
On his face,
And remembering/knowing
His reluctance
To spend time
With fans
And sycophants,
I pay attention to the road,
Thinking about
All the things I'd like to ask:

"How could you stick to
This writing game
For so long, nearly 40 years
Of your life,
With success
Coming so late?"
(And as I think this question,
I realize,
Maybe one day I'll ask myself the same thing,
Maybe it'll be equally true for me?)

I think of another question:
"When did you know that
Your wife Jordan
Was the last woman
You'd need to love
And that
Because she loved you too,
You needed to love her fully?"
(But I wonder
Will Gabrielle be my Jordan?
It's too early to know for sure…
Yet…)

And one final question:
"Was there a moment

In your writing
When you suddenly
Knew
You had it now,
That your dreams had shifted from
Something silly
(fame, $, recognition)
To something greater
And more real?"
But of course
This question
Would be
Rhetorical,
And Cole would answer,
"Have you read my work?
Just read it."
And I'd have to admit,
"I already have."
And he'd ask,
"So why the question?"
And I'd answer
In silence,
'Just because you're here
And I'm so happy to be with you,
And it's so damn quiet in this car.'
And he'd smile

And answer back
Solely by an equal measure of silence,
'There you go.'

And we'd drive on.
And the tires on the road would hum
And the cows in the field,
Grazing,
Wouldn't even glance up
As we moved past them.

And the silence
Would soon
Feel not just okay
But
Just right.

"Hand me a beer," he'd say to me.
And I'd pull one out and answer,
"Sure, Cole, here you go."
He'd twist off the cap
And toss it onto the floor
And look at me, a bit sheepishly,
And staring at the bottle cap,
He'd say, "Sorry about that…"
But then he'd smile

And take a big swig.
And I'd say,
"Don't worry about it,"
And we'd just keep going.

What a great ride.
What a cool day.
And to think,
I'll always have it.
The planet is round,
And this particular road
Never ends.
We'll just keep
Travelling,
Forever like this.

Acknowledgements

A number of people helped see this story to its final form: George Nicholson (RIP), Antonia Markiet of HarperCollins Children's Books, Will Weaver and Don Gallo who provided excellent advice, Russ Davis of Gray Dog Press, Jon Gosch of Latah Books, and Neil Clemons of Skyzblue Arts. If you enjoyed the story, these great folks deserve much of the credit; if you didn't like it, blame me.

Note: The poems presented in this work are originals by the author. *Uncle Walt, Unable, Walt Whitman and the Sparrows* (adapted from *Sparrows*) and *Riding with Cole* (adapted from *Riding With Buk.*) are all from the 2015 collection of poems *Where's the Fire?* This novel was originally planned as an homage in roman à clef to Charles Bukowski, thus the dedication.

Terry Trueman is the author of many books of fiction, non-fiction and poetry. He is best known as the Printz Honor Author of *Stuck in Neutral* (HarperCollins 2000). He has an MS in Applied Psychology and an MFA in Creative Writing. The father of two sons, Trueman is married and lives in Washington State.

For more information about Terry's work, visit his Wikipedia page or www.terrytrueman.com.